YOU ONLY DIE
TWICE

DAN GUTMAN

THE GENIUS FILES

YOU ONLY DIE TWICE

HARPER
An Imprint of HarperCollinsPublishers

Library of Congress Cataloging-in-Publication Data is available.
ISBN 978-0-06-182770-9 (trade bdg.)
ISBN 978-0-06-182771-6 (lib. bdg.)

Art and typography by Erin Fitzsimmons
13 14 15 16 17   CG/RRDH   10 9 8 7 6 5 4 3 2 1

First Edition

To Suzanne Daghlian, Maggie Herold, Esilda Kerr,
Andrea Pappenheimer, Cara Petrus, Robin Pinto,
Patti Rosati, Caroline Sun, Kimberly VandeWater,
and all the folks who work behind the scenes

"A grave is a grave."

—*Nobody said this. But somebody should have.*

To the Reader . . .

All the places mentioned in this book are real.

You can visit them. You *should* visit them!

Cont

ents

Thanks to Mona Banton of the National Jousting Association, Gail Bell, Jason Blau, Peter Blau, Diana Carr, Lisa Chapman, Joyce Allen-Crawford, Robert W. Dye, Esther Goldenberg, Ralph Hammelbacher, Andrew Harwell, Alan Kors, Samantha Kors, Beth Lucas, Brandon Lucas, Lee Ann Lucas, Megan Lucas, Zack Medlin, Jonathan Murdoch, Marcus Murdoch, Mike O'Connell, Andrew Paden, Lynne Paden, Andrea Reid, Sarah Saladini, John Shaffer of Luray Caverns, Angela Smith, Jon Van Hoozer, Jr., and Nina Wallace. A special thank-you to Google Maps and Roadside America.com, without which this book could not have been written.

There were ten items on Coke McDonald's to-do list for the month of July. But getting thrown into a giant shredder was not one of them.

CLEAN THE TOILET IN THE RV was on the list.

SEND POSTCARDS HOME was on the list.

BUY SOUVENIRS was on the list.

WORK ON SUMMER READING was on the list.

But nothing about getting thrown into a giant shredder.

And yet, oddly enough, getting thrown into a giant shredder was the *one* thing that Coke McDonald was actually going To Do during the month of July.

Wait a sec. Before I tell you how Coke McDonald was thrown into a giant shredder, it's really important for you to read a book called *The Genius Files: Never Say Genius*. Because if you didn't read *that* book, this one will make no sense at all. So ask your librarian for a copy, and read it. Then come back and start this one again. Fair enough?

Go ahead, I'll wait.

Hmmmm. Hmmmmmm. No rush or anything. I've got all day.

Okay, did you read it?

You did not!

Look, it's really important that you and I have an honest relationship during the time we're spending together between these covers. And if you can't be honest with me *here*, on page 2, what's it going to be like when we get to the big surprise ending on page 284?

DON'T YOU *DARE* TURN TO PAGE 284 TO SEE THE SURPRISE ENDING! How could you even *think* of doing such a terrible thing?

Look, just read the book, okay? What do you have to do that's more important? Watch some dumb reality TV show about people baking cakes? Watch videos of cats playing the piano on YouTube?

Okay, fine, don't read *The Genius Files: Never Say Genius*. See if I care.

Look, I'll make a deal with you. If you read *this* book, I'll tell you what happened in the last one in just eight breaths.

Deal?

Okay. This is what you missed. . . .

(Deep breath)

The story started on Coke and Pepsi McDonald's thirteenth birthday—June 25. The twins were still in shock after having pushed the evil and insane Dr. Herman Warsaw out of The Infinity Room to his death at The House on the Rock in Wisconsin. They were happy with the lame birthday presents their clueless parents gave them—a bag of genuine Wisconsin cheese curds and two yellow foam cheeseheads.

The family continued on their cross-country journey that had started in California, heading for their aunt Judy's wedding in Washington, D.C., on July 4.

Mrs. McDonald runs a popular website called *Amazing but True*. So along the way, she insisted on stopping at oddball tourist attractions, such as the National Mustard Museum (where she purchased a POUPON U toilet seat) and the National Dairy Hall of Fame (where the family learned about pioneers such

as Harvey D. Thatcher, the inventor of the glass milk bottle).

Wow, too bad you didn't read the book. You actually might have *learned* something!

(Deep breath)

Anyway, when they arrived at the first McDonald's restaurant in Des Plaines, Illinois, Coke and Pep encountered Archie Clone, a fellow teenage genius filer who was in fact an evil madman who aspired to follow in Dr. Warsaw's footsteps. He invited them into what appeared to be an interactive exhibit called "The Multimedia World of French Fries," but was in fact a death trap. Seconds before Coke and his sister were dipped into boiling oil, Coke jammed his cheesehead into the gears to stop the ridiculously slow-moving wire basket and save their lives.

Some birthday, huh?

(Deep breath)

The next stop was a Cubs game in Chicago's famed Wrigley Field, where Coke and Pep were reunited with the germ-phobic Mrs. Higgins, a hired assassin who worked for Dr. Warsaw when she wasn't teaching health at Coke and Pep's school back in California. She had given up killing innocent children, she said, and taken a job in the Cubs' public relations department (she has excellent people skills, apparently).

Mrs. Higgins told the twins there was a bomb in the Cubs' dugout that would go off when they sang the last line to "Take Me Out to the Ballgame." It was a lie, of course, but the result was that the entire ballpark had to be evacuated and the game forfeited to the hated St. Louis Cardinals. The twins were forced to run for their lives out of Wrigley, chased by an angry mob of frustrated Cubs fans, whose team usually finds a way to lose without any outside help.

Mrs. Higgins, by the way, also revealed that she was madly in love with Dr. Warsaw. So she was doubly furious with the twins because they killed her "boyfriend," and now it is highly unlikely that he will ever marry her.

Still with me? Good.

(Deep breath)

Continuing east from Chicago, the McDonald family stopped off to see Michael Jackson's boyhood home in Gary, Indiana; the largest egg in the world in Mentone, Indiana; and a pair of pants worn by the tallest man in the world.

You would think that Cedar Point, one of the greatest amusement parks in the *world*, would be nothing but fun. But it was there, in Sandusky, Ohio, where the twins were kidnapped off a roller coaster by two dudes in bowler hats and tied up in a Mister Softee

truck, where Archie Clone (who has a thing about food) poured soft-serve ice cream over their heads in an attempt to freeze them to death. Fortunately, Coke was able to cut the ropes with the sharp edge of the Pez dispenser he had hidden in his back pocket.

Whew, you sure missed a lot of stuff! You might want to seriously go back and read the book. I'm barely scratching the surface here.

(Deep breath)

After a quick stop in Avon, Ohio (the duct tape capital of the world), the McDonalds spent a day at the Rock and Roll Hall of Fame in Cleveland, where they were trapped in a recording studio and forced to listen to Megadeath at a volume meant to cause one's head to literally *explode.* Lucky they had picked up some duct tape in Avon! They were able to wrap it over their ears, punch a hole in the glass roof, and slide down the side of the pyramid-shaped building.

(Deep breath)

Their dad, Dr. McDonald, who is a history professor, decided to write his next scholarly book about President Herbert Hoover. He was thrilled to learn that the Hoover Historical Center was right down the road in North Canton, Ohio. But when they got there, they discovered that the Hoover Historical Center is devoted to *William* Hoover, the guy who started the Hoover Vacuum Cleaner Company! And like a vacuum cleaner, that really sucked.

Got all that?

Oh, I forgot to mention, the twins also visited a hot dog bun museum, the Spy Museum, and the largest collection of outhouses in the world. Plus, Coke got sprayed with poison gas in a highway rest stop bathroom by a guy wearing cowboy boots and whistling "The Yellow Rose of Texas." You'll have to read the book to get the details on all that stuff. No time for it here.

(Deep breath)

Finally, after deciphering a series of increasingly complicated secret messages, the twins were led to the Museum of American History in Washington, D.C. There they met up again with their nemesis, Archie Clone, along with his henchmen, a SWAT team in ski masks. Archie's plan was to steal the museum's prize artifact—the top hat Abraham Lincoln wore on the night he was assassinated.

Archie Clone dragged Coke and Pep up to the roof of the museum, where his helicopter was waiting. His plan was to kill the twins by dropping them on the tip of the Washington Monument. But at the last possible moment, they jumped out of the chopper and Pep

threw a Frisbee grenade to blow up Archie Clone's helicopter, killing him in a giant fireball.

Ouch! That's gotta hurt.

(Deep breath)

Did I mention that *The Genius Files: Never Say Genius* is totally inappropriate for children? Really, now that I've had the chance to think things over, it's *good* that you didn't read the book. It would have corrupted your innocent mind.

Anyway, the story ended the next day, with Aunt Judy's big wedding in Washington. And guess who she married?

Spoiler alert! It was Dr. Warsaw, the lunatic who was trying to kill Coke and Pep the whole time!

Ha! Betcha didn't see *that* coming! Yeah, it turns out that Dr. Warsaw survived the fall at The House on the Rock. Life, and death, can be funny that way.

So that's what happened. Whew! Let's see *you* try to sum up a 288-page book in eight breaths.

In any case, now you're up to speed. You're probably anxious to read *this* book to find out what happens to the McDonald twins next. Now that we got all that preliminary nonsense out of the way, let's get to the cool part—the part where Coke gets

thrown into a giant shredder.

So turn the page and get started. Because if you don't read this book, *The Genius Files #4* is going to make *no* sense at all.

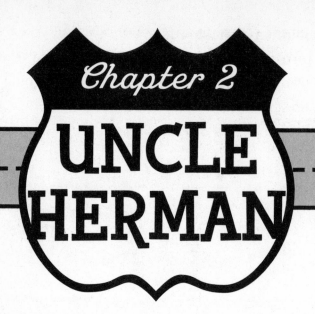

Chapter 2
UNCLE HERMAN

O   ur story begins in Washington, D.C., where
The Genius Files: Never Say Genius left off. By
the way, if you'd like to follow the McDonalds on their journey, it's easy. Get on the internet and go to Google Maps (http://maps.google.com/), Mapquest (www.mapquest.com), Rand McNally (www.randmcnally.com), or whatever navigation website you like best.

Go ahead, I'll wait.

Okay, now type in Lincoln Memorial, Washington, D.C., and click SEARCH MAPS. Click the little + or

– sign on the screen to zoom in or out until you get a sense of where the twins are. See it? That's our starting point.

It was July 4th, a beautiful sun-drenched afternoon in the nation's capital. The temperature outside was almost ninety, but you couldn't ask for a better day to have a wedding. The sad eyes of Abraham Lincoln looked down over the one hundred or so guests.

"Do you, Judy McAllister, take this man to be your husband in the holy state of matrimony? Will you love him, comfort him, honor and keep him, in sickness and in health, for richer, for poorer, for better, for worse, in sadness and in joy, as long as you both shall live?"

"I will," Aunt Judy said quietly.

Coke turned to look at his mother, who was beaming. She and Judy, her little sister, had not always gotten along while they were growing up. But all was forgiven now.

The minister turned to face the groom, who was sitting in a wheelchair.

"And do you, Herman Warsaw, take this woman to be your wife in the holy state of matrimony? Will you love her, comfort her, honor and keep her, in sickness and in health, for richer, for poorer, for better, for worse, in sadness and in joy, as long as you both shall live?"

"I do."

"By the power vested in me by the District of Columbia, I pronounce you husband and wife. You may kiss the bride."

For a moment or two, Coke and Pep didn't quite grasp what they had just heard. Did that minister really say "Herman Warsaw"?

It couldn't be! Dr. Warsaw was dead. Coke had personally karate kicked him out of The Infinity Room back in Wisconsin a week earlier. It had been hundreds of feet up in the air. There was no way he could have survived the fall. And besides, they had seen Dr. Warsaw's obituary in the newspaper. Maybe this guy was a different Herman Warsaw.

But no, there he was, sitting in a wheelchair.

All decked out in a tuxedo.

And getting married.

Kissing.

Aunt Judy.

As smart as they were, it took another moment or two for Coke and Pep to fully process the information. Dr. Warsaw was the reason they had been forced to jump off a cliff near their home in California. He was the reason they were locked in a burning school, pushed into a sand pit, and nearly drowned in a vat of bubbling Spam. It was because of him that they were zapped with electric shocks, lowered into boiling oil, and chased through the streets of Chicago. If Aunt Judy was their mother's sister, and she was marrying Dr. Warsaw, then that meant that Dr. Warsaw was now . . .

Uncle Herman!

They were related! Dr. Warsaw would be part of their family! How do you sit around the table on Thanksgiving with the man who tried to kill you?

Pep's jaw dropped open, and the blood drained from her face.

"Are you okay, sweetie?" asked her father. "You're white as a ghost."

That's when Pep's eyes rolled back in her head, and she collapsed.

Chapter 3

NOW IT'S PERSONAL

"We need a doctor over here!"

People were hollering for help before Pep had even hit the ground.

She was unconscious, lying on the grass, for about thirty seconds. When she opened her eyes, a doctor was leaning over her—Dr. Herman Warsaw.

Women, for unexplained reasons, found him irresistible. He was an odd-looking man. Extremely thin and squinty eyed, Dr. Warsaw was a chain smoker who dressed in baggy suits that made it look like he belonged in an old gangster movie. Years before, he had been a brilliant inventor who made a fortune with a GPS for people to track down their lost pets. A millionaire many times over, he got bored with making money and turned his attention to solving society's problems by enlisting the young people of the world. Then, of course, came 9/11, when the seeds of his insanity were germinated.

"She'll be okay," Dr. Warsaw proclaimed. "The heat must have gotten to her. She just needs a little air."

He had actually climbed down from his wheelchair to sit on the grass next to Pep. Somebody handed him a water bottle, and he put it to her lips, cradling her head in his arms like she was an injured puppy.

"What an adorable young lady," he said.

Pep, too petrified to move or speak, just stared at him, eyes wide-open. Coke watched from a few feet away, dumbfounded, as his sister was being nursed back to health by the man who had repeatedly tried to murder them.

Dr. Warsaw seemed to have matters well in hand, so the other grown-ups drifted away into small groups to do what grown-ups love to do—make small talk. Catch up. Introduce each other. Discuss the weather, as if it mattered. Mrs. McDonald ran over to hug Aunt Judy and congratulate her.

When the other grown-ups had become sufficiently

distracted, Dr. Warsaw lowered his voice so only the twins could hear.

"So we meet again," he whispered, his voice dripping with hatred. "I should just choke your sister to death right now, Coke."

"And I should just throw you on that wheelchair and push it down the steps," Coke said, "but that wouldn't look very good in front of all the relatives."

"I never expected you two to make it this far," Dr. Warsaw said quietly. "I thought I had gotten rid of you back in Cleveland at the Rock and Roll Hall of Fame. I'll say one thing about you brats. You are quite resourceful."

"And I thought *you* were dead at The House on the Rock after we pushed you out of The Infinity Room," Pep croaked.

"I almost was, thanks to you little punks!" Dr. Warsaw whispered. "Just about every bone in my body broke when I hit the ground. The doctors say I may never walk again."

"Boo-hoo," Coke said sarcastically.

"We were just defending ourselves!" Pep protested. "You were trying to kill *us*."

"Yes, and after that you killed my protégé, Archie. I spent years training that fine young man to carry on with my work. He was the son I never had."

Tears welled up in Dr. Warsaw's eyes as he talked about Archie Clone.

"He was trying to kill us too!" Pep pointed out. "He was going to drop us on the tip of the Washington Monument!"

"Oh, it's always about *you*, isn't it?" Dr. Warsaw sputtered, his face clenched. "Well, listen to me, you spoiled brats, and listen good. The differences between us have nothing to do with The Genius Files program anymore. Now it's personal."

"Wh-what are you gonna do to us?" Pep asked.

"Right now, sadly, I am in no condition to do anything to you," Dr. Warsaw told them. "But these broken bones will heal soon enough. And when they do, I'm going to track you down like dogs and make you pay for what you did to me and my young friend Archie. Believe me, you're going to wish you never tangled with me."

"We *already* wish we never tangled with you," Pep said. "You started it!"

"Don't argue with him," Coke told his sister, "He's insane!"

"Perhaps," Dr. Warsaw said. "Insanity and genius often go hand in hand."

"Let's blow this pop stand," Pep said as she stood up and brushed the grass off her dress.

Dr. Warsaw grabbed her wrist roughly before she could get away.

"Oh, and by the way," he said, "if you say one word about any of this to your parents, I will kill them both. I don't care if we're all related now. Mark my words. You know I do not make idle threats."

The other grown-ups, having run out of small talk, straggled back to get their belongings and say their good-byes. Mrs. McDonald and Aunt Judy were arm in arm, reminiscing about their childhoods.

"I'm so glad the whole family was able to be here for our special day!" said Aunt Judy.

"We wouldn't have missed it for the world," replied Mrs. McDonald. "You two seem so happy together."

"It was love at first sight," Aunt Judy gushed. "The second I set eyes on Hermy, I knew I had met the kindest, sweetest, most wonderful man in the world."

"You are *too* kind, my love," said Dr. Warsaw as he pulled himself back onto the wheelchair.

"Hermy?" asked Coke.

Pep looked like she might pass out again.

"You okay, Pep?" asked her father.

"I'll survive," she said.

Dr. Warsaw let out a nervous laugh.

"I'm glad you had the chance to meet our children,"

said Mrs. McDonald. "Now that you and I are family and everything."

"Yeah, family," muttered Coke. "One big, happy family."

"You have two lovely children," Dr. Warsaw said, pinching Pep's cheek just a little harder than necessary. "We had a nice chat just now. I look forward to getting together again very soon."

"Maybe after our honeymoon is over," added Aunt Judy. "We're going to California."

"Well, that's perfect!" said Dr. McDonald. "So are we!"

After lots of hugs and kisses all around, Aunt Judy wheeled Dr. Warsaw over to a van that had been specially outfitted with a wheelchair lift. She helped him inside. A dozen cans had been tied with string to the rear bumper and the words JUST MARRIED were written on the back window. All the guests gathered around to wave their good-byes and good wishes to the happy couple while the strains of Elvis Presley's "Love Me Tender" played in the background.

As Aunt Judy was starting up the van, Dr. Warsaw turned his head to make eye contact one last time with Coke and Pep. And as the van was pulling away, he glared at them with the evil eye.

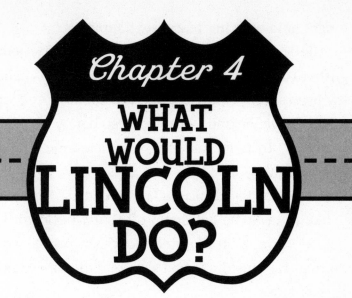

Chapter 4
WHAT WOULD LINCOLN DO?

"**W**hat are we gonna do *now*?" Pep asked her brother as the happy newlyweds drove away.

"I don't know," Coke said glumly.

"Why do you think Aunt Judy would marry a monster like Dr. Warsaw?" Pep asked.

"Why did Eva Braun marry Hitler?" Coke replied. "Why did Osama Bin Laden have three wives? Why do murderers get marriage proposals in prison? Some women like bad guys."

Standing just ten feet away, their mother could no

longer hold back her tears—of happiness.

"Didn't Aunt Judy look beautiful?" Mrs. McDonald gushed, dabbing her eyes with a tissue. "I can't believe my little sister is married. She was radiant. And what a great guy! She and Hermy look so happy together."

Hermy. To Coke and Pep, his nickname sounded like a disease.

"He seems like a nice fella," agreed Dr. McDonald. "I like the way he got down off that wheelchair and helped Pep after she fainted. Not many people would do that. He must have had a lot of experience taking care of kids."

Coke and Pep looked at each other in disbelief.

"Yeah," Coke said, "I bet he's taken care of a lot of kids."

Mrs. McDonald blew her nose into a handkerchief and seemed to be regaining her composure.

"I feel so sorry for Hermy," she said. "Judy told me he had an accident recently. He broke just about every bone in his body. That's why he was in a wheelchair."

"What happened?" asked Dr. McDonald.

"He took a bad fall."

Coke leaned over to whisper in Pep's ear. "Not bad enough."

After several more minutes, the grown-ups had finished chit-chatting, performing air kisses, and making false promises to stay in touch with each other. The wedding guests started to go their separate ways. Dr. McDonald led the family up the steps for a closer look at the Lincoln Memorial.

When they reached the top, the twins stared up in

wonder, like every other tourist visiting the shrine for the first time. It isn't until you get close to the statue of our sixteenth president that you realize how imposing it is.

"It's nineteen feet high," Coke told the family, "and it weighs 175 tons. The sculptor's name was Daniel Chester French."

"Get a life, Mr. Know-It-All," said Pep.

"Be nice to your brother," warned Mrs. McDonald.

It's not easy growing up with a twin who knows *everything*. From a very young age, Coke had been blessed with an eidetic—or photographic—memory. Whether he wanted to or not, he could remember virtually everything he ever read, saw, or heard. To some people, that made Coke an interesting and informed young man. To others, he was an obnoxious blowhard. Sometimes it seemed like his mouth was an endless fountain of useless information, a human search engine with no delete button.

Dr. McDonald smiled quietly. As a professor of American history at San Francisco State University, he took a secret delight in Coke's mental prowess.

"French's original plan called for the statue to be ten feet tall," he informed the others, "but he made it bigger so Lincoln wouldn't be dwarfed by his own monument."

The parents went to read the inscriptions that were carved in the north and south chambers of the memorial. The twins continued staring at Lincoln, who looked down at them with sad eyes.

"Did you know that five weeks after he became president, the Civil War began?" Coke told his sister. "And then, five days after the war was over, he was assassinated."

"It kinda makes our little everyday problems seem trivial," Pep said.

"People have been trying to assassinate us too," Coke reminded her. "That doesn't seem trivial to me."

He was right, and Pep knew it. She couldn't stop looking at the statue. It was like she was trying to make eye contact with a block of marble.

"What do you think Lincoln would do?" Pep finally asked her brother, "I mean, if he was in our shoes?"

"I wish I knew," he muttered.

They walked around the memorial to read the inscriptions on the walls. Coke and Pep were both familiar with the Gettysburg Address ("Four score and seven years ago . . ."), but neither of them had ever heard Lincoln's Second Inaugural Address. They read it all the way through to the end. . . .

With malice toward none; with charity for all; with firmness in the right, as God gives us to see the right, let us strive on to finish the work we are in; to bind up the nation's wounds; to care for him who shall have borne the battle, and for his widow, and his orphan— to do all which may achieve and cherish a just and lasting peace among ourselves, and with all nations.

"We should keep on going," Coke told his sister. "*That's* what Lincoln would do. We've got to stick together and strive to finish the work we're in."

Pep agreed, and the twins hugged each other.

A bunch of tourists were milling around, and a tour guide holding a little American flag was reading from her guidebook to a group of senior citizens gathered around her.

"As an enduring symbol of freedom," she told them, "the Lincoln Memorial attracts anyone who seeks inspiration and hope."

"That's what *we* need," Pep whispered to her brother. "Inspiration and hope."

"Yeah," Coke replied, "inspiration, hope . . . and a couple of those Frisbee grenades might come in handy too."

Chapter 5

A MESSAGE IN THE SKY

At this point, you're probably wondering when Coke McDonald is going to be thrown into a giant shredder. You may, in fact, be angry that he hasn't been thrown into a giant shredder *yet*. Patience, dear reader! Our story is just beginning. Good things come to those who wait. A promise is a promise, and my promise to you is that before this story is over, Coke will most certainly be thrown into a giant shredder.

The McDonald family walked north from the Lincoln Memorial, stopping to pay their respects at the Vietnam Veterans Memorial. Then they crossed Constitution Avenue and wandered around the side streets for a few minutes until they found a little Italian restaurant for an early dinner.

Pep was still a bit nervous and on edge about everything that had happened to her up to this point. But oddly enough Coke, who remembered *everything*, had a way of putting the bad experiences out of his mind and looking toward the future. He was starting to relax.

And why shouldn't he? Dr. Warsaw was away on his honeymoon with Aunt Judy. He couldn't do anything to harm anybody. Even if that lunatic wanted to, he was severely injured and in a wheelchair. It would be a long time before he'd be able to walk, much less hurt innocent children.

By the time Dr. Warsaw's broken bones healed, Coke figured, they'd be back home in California and could deal with him then. In the meantime, they might as well enjoy themselves while they could. That was Coke's attitude.

"Are you kids excited about the fireworks tonight?" Dr. McDonald asked as he bit into his second slice of pizza.

"You know it!" Coke shouted, giving his dad a high five. He had nearly forgotten that it was the Fourth of

July and that there was a big fireworks display on the National Mall.

It's a fact that making stuff is interesting. Taking stuff apart is also interesting. But destroying stuff and blowing stuff up is *cool*. It doesn't matter what it is—firecrackers, cherry bombs, M-80s, bottle rockets, Roman candles, mortar shells. Anything you can light up that will explode with noise, light, smoke, flames, and flying debris is cool. Coke and his dad had a gleam in their eyes just thinking about the fireworks.

It's a guy thing.

That's sexist, I know. And there are exceptions, of course. But in general, it could be said that girls like fuzzy bunnies, puppies, and kittens, while guys like throwing water balloons at each other and setting Ping-Pong balls on fire. Girls get pleasure from shopping and trying on new clothes. Guys prefer watching cars crash into each other at high speed.

I could go on, but you get the idea. We're different. Nothin' wrong with that.

Dr. McDonald paid for dinner, and the family walked back to the National Mall. It was already getting crowded on the grass. Some people had camped out for hours so they would get the best view of the fireworks, next to the reflecting pool between the

29

Lincoln Memorial and the World War II Memorial.

Mrs. McDonald found an open spot and spread a blanket on the grass. A few kids were throwing footballs around, so Coke pulled his Frisbee out of his backpack and flipped it to his sister. They moved off to the side to have a catch.

"Fireworks were invented in seventh-century China to frighten evil spirits, y'know," Coke informed his sister. "They would roast bamboo to create a loud bang that would scare away imaginary one-footed monsters."

"Do tell more, O wise one," Pep said, rolling her eyes as she purposely flung the Frisbee over her brother's head to make him go chase it.

Ever since they left California, she had been getting better and better. Now Pep could effortlessly whip a Frisbee long distances with nearly pinpoint accuracy. She was better than her brother, not that he would ever admit that.

"Did you know," Coke told her, "that a simple sparkler can get as hot as one thousand degrees Fahrenheit? You can actually melt gold at that temperature."

"I was being sarcastic," Pep replied. "I didn't *really* want to hear any more about fireworks."

"Why not?" he replied. "They're gonna shoot up

thirty-three tons of explosives out here tonight! Can you imagine? Thirty-three tons of potassium, zinc, titanium, sulfur, and phosphorus, igniting and exploding before our eyes! How awesome is that gonna be?"

"Awesomely awesome," Pep said with zero enthusiasm.

"Y'know," Coke continued, "I heard about some guy who was shooting off rockets in his backyard on the Fourth of July last year. One of them didn't fire right away, so he looked into the tube to see what was wrong. Then the thing fired and it blew his head off! It blew it clean off! He was still standing there five seconds later with no head!"

"Will you *shut up* already?" Pep shouted. She stopped tossing the Frisbee.

"Okay, okay!" Coke said. "What's your problem?"

"It's just that I have a bad feeling—"

Uh-oh. *Feelings.* Those things that girls have. Coke couldn't relate.

"—I have a feeling something's going to happen during the fireworks show," Pep admitted. "Something bad."

"Like what?" Coke asked. "Dr. Warsaw is on his honeymoon. He's not going to bother us here."

"What about those bowler dudes?" Pep asked. "They got away in the helicopters. Who knows where

they are? And what about Mrs. Higgins? That nutcase is still running around. She could be watching us through binoculars right *now* for all we know."

Coke scanned the perimeter of the Mall, looking for snipers on the rooftops.

"What are any of them gonna do?" he asked, satisfied that they were safe.

"Oh, gee, I don't know," Pep said, her voice drenched in sarcasm. "Let me think. There will be thirty-three tons of chemicals exploding in close proximity to thousands of people. What could a crazy person possibly do? Blow up the Lincoln Memorial? Knock down the Washington Monument? Lob a bomb in the middle of all these people? There are plenty of things they could do!"

"I doubt that—" Coke began.

"Don't you see?" Pep continued. "The Fourth of July is the perfect time for a crazy person to attack us, or *all* these people. The sky will be lit up with explosions. Nobody would know if there was a *real* bomb going off at the same time. They'd think it was part of the show."

"Hmmm, I never thought of that," Coke admitted.

Pep could see the tide was turning. She was winning the argument.

"Look," she said, "we blew up Archie Clone's helicopter at the Museum of American History. Wasn't that enough fireworks for you?"

"That *was* cool," Coke admitted. "Okay, I see your point. Maybe we should get out of here, just to be on the safe side. Let's go talk it over with Mom and Dad."

The twins went back to the blanket, where their parents were cuddling.

"Ugh, gross!" Coke exclaimed, "Will you two knock it off before I get sick? We don't need to see that."

"What's up, offspring?" asked Dr. McDonald as he untangled himself from Mrs. McDonald.

"We're tired," Pep explained. "Maybe we should call it a night."

"Yeah, we don't want to stick around for the fireworks," Coke said. "Let's blow this pop stand."

"What?!" both parents exclaimed.

"Call it a night? Are you crazy?" Dr. McDonald roared. "We're in Washington. It's the Fourth of July. Of *course* we're going to watch the fireworks. It's a tradition. It's patriotic. It's American."

"Can't we just watch them on TV?" Pep suggested.

"Are you kids coming down with something?" Mrs. McDonald asked as she reached over to touch their foreheads. "You always loved fireworks back home."

"We've seen them a million times," Coke told his parents. "It's always the same. Bang. Boom. Flash. Big finale. The end."

"We're staying right here, and that's the last—"

At that moment, there was a huge explosion in the sky above. While the McDonalds had been arguing about whether or not to stick around and watch the fireworks, darkness had fallen on the Mall. The show had begun.

"Oooooooooooooh!" moaned the crowd as the first rocket reached its apogee and exploded in fiery tentacles of red, white, and blue. All eyes turned upward. The National Symphony Orchestra struck up a John Philip Sousa march to accompany the visual display as another rocket was launched. It exploded with a *BOOM* and lit up the sky with white light. Nobody was going to leave now.

"Be ready," Coke whispered to his sister.

He pulled a baseball cap over his face and scanned the crowd, looking for guys in bowler hats, evil health teachers, wheelchair-bound lunatics, or anything suspicious. The Mall was jammed with thousands of people now, and any of them could be up to no good.

"Oooooooooooooh!" moaned the crowd as ten rockets went up at once. The resulting flash illuminated the Washington Monument in a multicolor display that was as pretty as a postcard. Hundreds of cell phones were pointed at the sky. You couldn't help but feel like you were Francis Scott Key watching the rockets' red glare, the bombs bursting in air over Fort

McHenry during the War of 1812.

"You kids don't have to sit with us if you don't want to," Mrs. McDonald told the twins. "We know what a drag it is at your age to hang out with parents."

"Yeah, go have a good time," Dr. McDonald said.

"We don't want to have a good time," Pep replied nervously. "We want to be with you."

Over the next half hour, the crowd *ooooh*ed and *ahhhh*ed, mesmerized by multicolored pinwheels, twirling circles, bursting stars, smiley faces, hearts,

clovers, and American flags lighting up the night. Rockets shot upward and painted the sky with glittery trails of sparks in the shape of waterfalls or weeping willow trees, only to fizzle out and vanish before their embers reached the ground. Little children covered their ears with their hands. The boomers, hummers, crackles, and high-pitched screaming whistles that echoed off the monuments were just too much stimulation for their fragile eardrums.

If you closed your eyes, it sounded like a war was going on and you were in the middle of the battlefield. The pyrotechnic display was awe inspiring, if you weren't thinking the whole time that you were about to have a bomb drop on your head. Pep went into the fetal position on the ground. She was shaking with fear.

When the orchestra kicked into Tchaikovsky's "1812 Overture," everyone knew it was time for the finale. The U.S. Army Herald Trumpets joined in, as did cannon fire from the United States Army Presidential Salute Battery.

With the final crescendo, dozens of rockets shot up and exploded into the night, leaving only these letters hanging in the sky . . .

And then all was quiet.

"Huh?" the crowd seemed to ask as one.

"What's that mean?" somebody asked.

"They must have spelled something wrong," said Mrs. McDonald.

The meaningless letters hung in the air for a few seconds until they gradually faded away in a twinkling of white sparks.

The show was over. There was a moment of silence, followed by wild applause and cheering. People started to pick up their lawn chairs, blankets, coolers, and trash.

Coke and Pep didn't clap or cheer. They just felt relief. There had been no *real* bombs. Nobody had died.

"Did you just see what I just saw?" Pep whispered to her brother as they followed the crowd to the exit.

"That depends on what you just saw," he replied.

"I just saw some letters that didn't make any sense."

"Me too," replied Coke, who had already memorized the message in the sky. "Do you think it was just a mistake?"

"No," Pep told him. "I think it was a cipher."

Go to Google Maps (http://maps.google.com/).

Click Get Directions.

In the A box, type Washington D.C.

In the B box, type Culpeper VA.

Click Get Directions.

Chapter 6

THE BATTLE OF CEDAR MOUNTAIN

A cipher is a secret message, usually one that can be decoded by substituting or changing the order of the letters. Ever since Coke and Pep left California, they had been receiving a new cipher every few days.

At first the ciphers were coming from Dr. Warsaw. After his "accident," they were sent by his young madman-in-training, Archie Clone. But Dr. Warsaw was on his honeymoon, and Archie Clone was dead. Who could be sending the twins ciphers *now*? And what could LEVEL VIS I possibly mean?

Pep wasn't very good at remembering vast quantities of information like her brother. But she was excellent at analyzing data, and she made a study of it. She had an uncanny ability to take a series of seemingly random letters, numbers, or symbols and rearrange them to reveal their secret meaning.

"What does LEVEL VIS I mean?" Coke whispered impatiently as they followed their parents to the Metro station.

"I don't know yet!" Pep replied. "Give me a break, will you? I need to work on it."

By the time they took the train back to the campground, checked out, and made it through the traffic jam getting out of Washington, it was past midnight. The kids had nearly fallen asleep. But they both woke up when the RV crossed the Arlington Memorial Bridge and a sign appeared at the side of the road.

"Woo hoo!" Coke hooted. "The Old Dominion State! Did you guys know that the Revolutionary War and the Civil War *both* ended in Virginia?"

"I actually *did* know that," said Dr. McDonald from the driver's seat. "The Revolution ended with the surrender of Cornwallis in Yorktown. The Civil War ended at Appomattox."

"But I'll bet you didn't know that *eight* presidents were born in Virginia, Dad," Coke continued. "Washington, Jefferson, Madison, Monroe, Harrison, Tyler, Taylor, and Wilson."

"Thank you, Mr. Boring," Pep told her brother.

"And the state beverage of Virginia is milk," Coke added, just to annoy her.

"Nobody cares, doofus."

"Don't call your brother a doofus," said Mrs. McDonald.

With Coke's help, Pep wrote LEVEL VIS I down in her notebook. She began to work on it, juggling the letters around in her head. This was a hard one. It was very late, and Pep was too tired. Soon the notebook and pen had dropped from her hand.

Coke was just about asleep too when Dr. McDonald pulled the RV onto Route 66 heading west. He drove silently for nearly an hour and a half, passing very close to the battlefield of Bull Run and Manassas,

splitting off south on Route 15 and 29.

Can you find it on the map? Go ahead, I'll wait.

It was close to two o'clock in the morning when the RV turned onto the gravel road at Cedar Mountain Campground in Culpeper, Virginia. Coke and Pep didn't wake up. Dr. McDonald parked the RV and checked in at the office. Then he climbed back in and was asleep almost as soon as his head hit the pillow.

"Rise and shine!" Mrs. McDonald hollered cheerfully the next morning, July 5.

"C'mon, kids," Dr. McDonald said, clapping his hands. "We've got three thousand miles to drive before we get back home again!"

Coke and Pep groaned and stumbled out of the RV, plopping themselves down at a picnic table for breakfast. Mrs. McDonald had prepared instant oatmeal. There is a fishing pond and other amenities at Cedar Mountain Campground, but it didn't look like they would get the chance to use them.

Dr. McDonald had spread out a road map of the United States that covered half the table. He leaned over it, stabbing his finger at the state of Virginia. He looked like a general planning out his next battle.

"Okay, we took a northern route from California to

get to Washington," he reminded the twins. "So we're going to take a southern route going back home. That way we can see a lot more cool stuff."

He traced a potential route with his finger down through Virginia, North Carolina, South Carolina, Georgia, Alabama, Mississippi, and across Texas through the west.

"Are we going to visit any more giant balls of twine?" Pep asked wearily.

"Of course not!" her mother replied. "Been there, done that. I just want to make sure we get to Paris, Texas, where they have a replica of the Eiffel Tower with a giant cowboy hat on top."

The twins rolled their eyes. Mrs. McDonald owned and operated a popular website called *Amazing but True* that focused on unusual and often ridiculous tourist destinations across the United States. On the trip east, she had insisted that they stop at museums devoted to yo-yos, mustard, Spam, and Pez dispensers. The family also had to visit *two* giant balls of twine—one in Cawker City, Kansas, and the other in Darwin, Minnesota.

Yes, all of these places actually exist. Go ahead and look them up if you don't believe me.

Dr. McDonald carefully folded up his map.

"I chose this campground because the Battle of Cedar Mountain took place just a few miles from here," he said. "The first thing we're going to do today is visit the battlefield."

"Why *this* one, Dad?" Coke asked. "There were over a hundred Civil War battles fought in Virginia."

"Well, you know what they say," Dr. McDonald told him, smiling. "You've got to choose your battles."

After cleaning up from breakfast and checking out of the campground, they drove a few miles south of Culpeper until they found the site of the Battle of Cedar Mountain. There isn't much there today. Just a large field and a few historical markers.

"During the Civil War," Dr. McDonald told the

family, "the capitals of the Union and the Confederacy were only about a hundred miles away from each other. This is just about the midpoint, so it made sense for them to have a battle here."

THE BATTLE OF
CEDAR MOUNTAIN

On August 9, 1862, a Confederate army under "Stonewall" Jackson fought a hot engagement here in the shadow of Cedar Mountain against a Federal force commanded by the brashly confident John Pope. Jackson's army was much stronger, but a bold Federal advance nearly routed the Confederates. When Jackson's reserves under A. P. Hill arrived they stabilized the front and then steadily drove the Union army from the field. Although his brilliant exploits as Lee's right arm were to continue for the nine remaining months of his life, Cedar Mountain was the last battle "Stonewall" commanded on his own.

ERECTED BY THE CULPEPER CAVALRY MUSEUM

Coke spotted something at the other end of the field.

"Look!" he shouted. "Some guys are fighting! Cool!"

Dr. McDonald parked the RV and the family ran over to find out what was going on. As they got closer, they could see soldiers in blue and gray uniforms running around, shooting, shouting, loading muskets, falling, and sometimes dying. Or so it seemed, anyway.

"It's a reenactment," Dr. McDonald yelled over the boom of a cannon. "These guys dress up in Union

and Confederate uniforms, and they act out the battle just as it happened back in 1862."

It was a hot day. Pep felt sorry for the "soldiers," who had to wear those heavy uniforms and run around carrying big muskets. Coke was entranced. If there's one thing more interesting than watching stuff explode, it's watching people pretending to shoot at each other.

The soldiers on both sides would advance and then form a wide line to aim and fire their muskets. It took about a minute for them to reload after each shot and fire again. Some of them fell to the ground. It was exciting and loud.

"It seems like a dumb way to fight," Coke commented.

"Remember, they didn't have airplanes and bombs and unmanned drones in those days," Dr. McDonald told him. "They fought the way they were told to fight, using the technology that was available at the time."

It was hard to tell who was winning. Soldiers on both sides were getting "hit" and dropping in their tracks. When the battle was over, the "dead" soldiers got up, brushed themselves off, and got a nice round of applause from the tourists who were milling around. The McDonalds and a few other families gathered around to chat with the reenactors. One of the Confederates explained that he participated in battle reenactments every few weekends to honor the soldiers who fought so hard during the Civil War and to keep their memory alive.

"Stonewall Jackson led our troops," he said. "Nine months later, the Battle of Chancellorsville took place not far from here. One of our guys mistook Stonewall for a Union officer and fired a volley at him. A bullet shattered his arm, and it had to be amputated just below the shoulder. Then they buried the arm in its own grave."

"Wow," Coke said, fascinated.

The reenactor told the twins that when Robert E. Lee heard what happened to Stonewall, he said, "He has lost his left arm, but I have lost my right."

"That's so sad," said Pep.

"Yeah, it was even sadder when Stonewall died eight days later," said the reenactor. "War ain't pretty, young lady. In fact, it's pretty ugly."

The show was over. It was odd to watch the Civil War reenactors pack up their gear and load it into minivans in the parking lot. The twins were hot and thirsty, and Dr. McDonald gave them a few dollars to buy cold drinks at a little snack truck. Coke and Pep got in line behind two people dressed as Union soldiers.

"What can I get you?" asked the lady in the truck.

"I'll have a Coke," said Coke.

"I'd like a Pepsi," said Pep.

They paid for their drinks and moved off to the side. But no sooner had they taken their first sips when two hands clapped over their faces.

"Keep your mouths shut!" a gruff voice muttered.

"But we didn't—"

"Shut up!"

Coke felt a pillowcase being pulled down over his head. His arms were pinned to his sides. He struggled to free himself, but there was nothing he could do. He felt himself being dragged into the woods.

"We're gonna die!" Pep tried to yell. "I knew it! We're gonna die!"

Chapter 7

THE COAST IS CLEAR

Coke and Pep were lowered to the ground more gently than they expected. When they ripped the pillowcases off their heads, their kidnappers had familiar faces.

"Bones!" shouted Coke.

"Mya!" shouted Pep.

Now, if you had read the first two Genius Files books, you would know that Bones and Mya are on the side of goodness and niceness. They once worked for Dr. Warsaw to start The Genius Files project but quit when he lost his mind and became determined to kill off all the children. At that point, they made it their mission to help Coke, Pep, and any other Genius Filers who were being pursued by Dr. Warsaw or his henchman.

That's okay, you know it now. The important thing is that Bones and Mya are friends and had already saved the twins' lives several times.

"What are you doing here?" Pep asked as she hugged them.

"We came to see you two," Mya told her. "We have good news."

"It's about time," Coke said.

"We've intercepted several text messages over the last few days," Bones reported, looking around to make sure they were alone. "Dr. Warsaw, it seems, is genuinely head over heels in love with your aunt Judy and is no longer interested in hurting children. Love will do that to a man. He's as harmless as a puppy dog now."

"And we've also heard that Mrs. Higgins and those bowler dudes are out of the assassination business," Mya said. "So you can rest easy."

Pep, for one, wasn't buying it.

"Can you trust those text messages you inter-cepted?" Pep asked.

"Yeah," Coke added, "how do we know there aren't any *new* enemies out to get us? Like that Archie Clone jerk. He came out of the woodwork."

"I can't offer any guarantees," Bones told them,

"but I'm pretty confident the coast is clear. You can live your lives. You don't need us anymore."

"Yeah, well, just in case, how about giving us something to defend ourselves?" asked Coke. "Like a few of those cool Frisbee grenades, like the one we used to blow up Archie Clone's helicopter?"

"We can't do that," Mya said, reaching into her handbag. "The Frisbee grenades cost fifty thousand dollars each. But we did bring you a little good-bye present."

She pulled out a small plastic jar with some kind of liquid inside.

"What is it?" Pep asked.

Mya unscrewed the top of the jar and pulled out a little black wand with a circle at the end. She dipped it into the liquid and blew on it. Bubbles floated through the air.

"You got us . . . *bubbles*?" Pep was incredulous.

"I know," Coke said. "They're probably *exploding* bubbles, right? You blow them into some bad guy's face and . . . boom . . . his *head* is blown off! That is ingenious! Thanks. I can't wait to try this out."

"Uh, they're not exploding bubbles," Bones said. "I'm sorry."

"No? Oh, I get it," said Coke. "The bubbles are filled with poison gas, right? You blow one and when it pops, your enemy inhales the gas and drops dead instantly, right? Cool! What will you people think of next?"

"There's no poison gas in the bubbles, Coke," Mya told him.

"Maybe the poison gas just puts you to sleep?" Coke suggested. "Or into a coma. That is *awesome*!"

"No, the only gas in the bubbles is oxygen," Mya explained. "They're just plain old *bubbles*. We picked them up in a gift shop. You blow them. They float around. They're pretty. We thought you'd like them. Just be careful not to get them in your eyes. The soap stings like the dickens."

"Gee, thanks a *lot*," Coke said, taking the jar. "Now that I have bubbles, I can defend the free world. I feel a lot safer."

"We already told you," Mya said, "the coast is clear. You don't have to worry anymore."

"What about the cipher we received?" Pep asked. "LEVEL VIS I. It was part of the Fourth of July fireworks show we saw in Washington."

"I don't think that's a cipher," Mya said. "It sounds more like a typo or something."

"Even if it was a cipher," Bones told them, "how do you know it was meant for *you*? There were thousands of people there yesterday. The message, if there was one, could have been intended for *anybody* in that crowd."

"I guess you're right," Pep said.

"Well, I just wanted to say that it has been a pleasure working with you two," Bones said. "Our job is done now. We wish you the best of luck in your future, wherever it may lead you."

After a group hug, the twins ran back to the RV, where their parents were waiting.

"Where were you two?" Mrs. McDonald said sternly. "You were just supposed to go get sodas. We were looking all over."

There was a time when the twins would tell a lie to get out of trouble, but that never worked. They would forget the lie they had told, or it would be proven not to be true. At some point, Coke decided it was simply easier to tell the truth.

"We were kidnapped by a couple of Union soldiers at the snack truck," he explained. "They put pillowcases over our heads and dragged us in the woods. Then they gave us this jar of soap bubbles."

"Ha ha! That's a good one," Dr. McDonald said. "You kids crack me up."

Go to Google Maps (http://maps.google.com/).

Click Get Directions.

In the A box, type Culpeper VA.

In the B box, type Luray VA.

Click Get Directions.

Chapter 8

A DIFFERENCE OF OPINION

"That Civil War reenactment was cool," Pep said as Dr. McDonald pulled the RV onto Route 522 out of Culpeper.

Mrs. McDonald smiled to herself as she leafed through her Virginia guidebook. She loved it when an activity she had chosen was enjoyable to the whole family. It's usually hard to please everybody, and especially the kids. They usually hated everything, or *said* they did, anyway.

It was close to noon, and the temperature had climbed past ninety. Dr. McDonald always tried to avoid running the air conditioner because it robbed the RV—which already guzzled gas—of mileage. But on this day, he shut the windows and turned up the AC. Coke and Pep munched on trail mix Mrs. McDonald had prepared earlier.

"Y'know, we should go to George Washington's home, Mount Vernon," suggested Dr. McDonald, "and Thomas Jefferson's home, Monticello. I don't think they're too far from here."

"*Everybody* goes to those places, Ben," Mrs. McDonald said dismissively.

"Everybody goes to those places because they're places worth *going* to," Dr. McDonald replied. "Do you know why the Pez museum and the Spam museum were so empty? Because nobody wants to go there. Nobody *cares* about Pez or Spam."

Coke and Pep sat in the back, pretending not to be drinking in every word. As you know, it's always interesting to listen to your parents fighting.

In any case, Mount Vernon and Monticello were not exactly on the route Mrs. McDonald had plotted out. They were heading west through Virginia now, on Route 522.

"Hey, guess what they have near Fredericksburg?" Mrs. McDonald suddenly asked.

"A lot of guys named Frederick?" Coke guessed.

"No," his mother said, "a tomb with Stonewall Jackson's arm in it!"

"His *arm*?" asked Pep.

"Yes! Remember they told us that his arm had to be amputated after he got shot in the Civil War? The soldier wasn't joking. The arm has its own grave near Fredericksburg."

"I guess they disarmed him," cracked Coke.

"Very funny," Dr. McDonald said.

"That would be great for *Amazing but True*, Mom," Pep said. "The burial site of an arm."

"Hey, do you think Stonewall Jackson read *A Farewell to Arms* before he died?" asked Coke.

"That book hadn't even been written when he died," Mrs. McDonald told him.

"It was a *joke*, Mom." Coke rolled his eyes. He made a mental note to work on his theory that after the age of thirty, the part of the brain that controls sense of humor withers away and dies.

"We should totally go there," Pep said. "I want to see it."

"We're heading *west*," Dr. McDonald said. "Fredericksburg is an hour east of here. I'm not driving an hour out of my way to see an arm."

"You can't see the arm itself, dear," Mrs. McDonald told him. "You would just see the gravesite where the arm is buried."

"Well, I'm not driving an hour out of my way to see the *gravesite* of an arm."

Mrs. McDonald sighed. Her website received over a million hits a week, which made her the main breadwinner of the family (that means she makes more money). Dr. McDonald was a history professor at San Francisco State University who wrote scholarly books

like *The Impact of Coal on the Industrial Revolution*. Sadly, the average person is more interested in Spam and Pez than they are in coal. It was the advertising revenue from *Amazing but True* that paid for the trip. So when it came to deciding what places they would visit, Mrs. McDonald usually called the shots.

But not this time. Dr. McDonald didn't put his foot down often, but when he did, there was no more argument. And he was doing all the driving, which counted for something.

"It's a *historic* arm, honey," Mrs. McDonald said, giving it one last try. "It's Stonewall Jackson's arm."

"I don't care if it's Vincent Van Gogh's ear!" Dr. McDonald said, raising his voice. "I'm not driving an hour out of my way to see the gravesite of a body part. If it was his *whole* body, maybe I'd think about it."

And that was the end of that.

But it was okay, because there are a lot of other amazing but true places in the state of Virginia. You probably don't know this, dear reader, but in Arlington, Virginia, there's an eighteen-foot-tall mermaid carved into a tree. In Bealeton, there's a giant roller skate outside a roller rink. There's a house built out of old tombstones in Petersburg. There's a big watering can outside a garden center in Alexandria. And the birthplace of George Washington's mother is in Alfonso.

"You have to set your priorities," Dr. McDonald kept repeating. "We can't see everything."

While his parents argued back and forth in the front seat, Coke blew some bubbles with the jar Bones and Mya had given him. Pep pulled out her notebook. She had been thinking about the cipher they received at the end of the Fourth of July fireworks, but so far had not been able to solve it. She stared at the letters again.

LEVEL VIS I

What could *that* mean? She tried all the usual code-breaking strategies—reverse letters, every other letter, every second letter. Nothing worked.

She sighed and put the notebook away. If Bones and Mya were right, it didn't matter anyway. Nobody was chasing them now. They could relax.

"Hit the brakes, Ben!" Mrs. McDonald suddenly shouted.

"What?" Dr. McDonald shouted, stomping his foot on the pedal. "Did we run over an animal?"

"No! Look!"

There was a large sign at the side of the road.

"Caves are cool," Coke said, "in more ways than one. Fifty-four degrees, twenty-four hours a day."

"Let's go!" Pep shouted.

They pulled into the parking lot. Dr. McDonald paid the admission and got four sets of audio guides, two for the kids and two for the grown-ups.

"Meet you in the gift shop at the end of the tour," Mrs. McDonald told the kids.

"How do you know there's going to be a gift shop, Mom?" Pep asked.

"There's *always* a gift shop."

Coke and Pep put on their headphones and walked down a long series of stairs, ramps, and brick paths until they had reached the entrance to the caverns, deep within the earth. It was pitch-dark except for some tiny lights on the floor to help people find their way. The twins held on to the handrail for safety.

"This place is creepy," Pep said. But Coke was listening to the lady's voice on the audio guide. . . .

You are about to enter Luray Caverns. Welcome. On the morning of August 13, 1878, a tinsmith named Andrew Campbell was walking with a candle on a hill west of Luray, Virginia. Suddenly, cold air rushing out of a limestone sinkhole blew out the candle. That was the day Luray Caverns was discovered.

"Does that voice sound familiar to you?" Pep asked her brother. But with his own headset on, he couldn't hear her.

The path turned a corner and opened up to a spellbinding sight—a gigantic "room" filled with majestic stalactites and stalagmites of all sizes. Multicolored lights had been strategically hidden to illuminate the rock formations and throw off spooky shadows. Some of the stalactites slowly dripped water into a "dream lake" that formed a mirror image of the formations above it. Coke and Pep stood there openmouthed. It was like a magical world.

The formations you see are calcite, a crystalline form of limestone. Caves result from a simple formula—a layer of limestone, a mildly acidic mixture of water and carbon dioxide, and time—millions of years.

"I could *swear* I've heard that voice before," Pep muttered.

They walked through several other chambers until they reached one that was called the Cathedral. In this room they found the Great Stalacpipe Organ, the world's largest musical instrument. The lady on the audio guide explained that it took thirty-six years to connect rubber-tipped mallets to hundreds of stalactites in this cave. When the mallets are struck, it creates a sound unlike anything else in the world.

The voice on the audio guide paused, and eerie, haunting music began to play all around them. The hairs on Pep's arm stood up. She was beginning to get one of those feelings she gets—the feeling that something was terribly wrong.

The twins were alone in the Cathedral Room. Or so they thought.

Coke felt a tap on his shoulder.

He turned around.

It was Mrs. Higgins.

Chapter 9

A PASSION FOR SPELUNKING

Yes, Mrs. Higgins—the germ-phobic and psychotic health teacher who had set the twins' school on fire, chased them through The House on the Rock, forced them to cause a riot at Wrigley Field in Chicago, and tried to blow their eardrums out at the Rock and Roll Hall of Fame in Cleveland! She still had a scar across her neck from when they had clotheslined her with a ball of twine in Wisconsin.

Coke and Pep involuntarily recoiled in horror at the sight of the tall woman, backing up against the clammy cave wall.

(I know what you're thinking, dear reader. You're thinking that Mrs. Higgins is going to throw Coke into a giant shredder. But that's not what happened at all.)

"Well, if it isn't the McDonald twins!" Mrs. Higgins said, smiling sweetly. "Fancy meeting you two here."

"It was *you*!" Pep said, pointing at her. "You're the voice on the audio tour!"

"Guilty as charged," she replied. "How did I sound?"

"Don't touch us!" Coke warned. "I'm warning you. I have a brown belt in karate."

"Congratulations," Mrs. Higgins said. "Don't worry. I never touch the visitors. That is strictly forbidden by company rules."

She took a step back and held up both hands to prove that she had no weapon.

"What are you doing here?" Pep demanded. "Why do you keep showing up wherever we go?"

"I work here, dear," Mrs. Higgins said. "I'm just trying to make a living. I got laid off when the school burned down, you know."

"You burned the school down *yourself*!" Coke shouted at her.

"Believe me, it's not easy getting a job these days," said Mrs. Higgins. "The economy is terrible."

"You can't fool us," Pep said. "You work for Dr. Warsaw. You're in love with him, and you'll do *anything*

he says to make him happy, including killing innocent kids. You're a paid assassin!"

Mrs. Higgins put her hand over her heart, as if taken aback by the accusation. She appeared to get misty-eyed at the mention of Dr. Warsaw's name.

"Okay, I did do a little, shall we say, *freelancing*, for Dr. Warsaw," she admitted. "But those days are over. He's married now, and I finally had to admit that he never really loved me in the first place. In the end, he had me stealing hats for that kid who looked like Archie from the comics. It was pathetic what I did for that man's approval, to be honest with you."

She wiped a tear from her eye, and Pep found herself feeling a small degree of sympathy for Mrs. Higgins. She almost wanted to give her a hug.

"She's lying," Coke told his sister. "Don't fall for that crap, Pep."

"I was going through a phase back then," Mrs. Higgins said, her eyes brightening. "But those days are in the past. Now I have a new passion—spelunking!"

"Spelunking?" Pep asked.

"Exploring caves."

"I don't believe you for a *second*," Coke said. "We trusted you the last time. And now we're supposed to believe that you just *happened* to get a job at Luray Caverns when we're here, just like you *happened* to get the job at Wrigley Field when we were in Chicago? Give me a break."

"You can believe whatever you want, Coke," said Mrs. Higgins. "But look, if I wanted to harm you two, I could do it right now, couldn't I?"

She turned around and made a sweeping gesture across the Cathedral Room with her arm.

"You see these stalagmites?" she continued. "Some of them are sharper than a razor. How easy it would be for me to grab one of you and push you down on top of one."

Mrs. Higgins had a glassy look in her eye. Coke and Pep took a step backward.

"That's all it would take," Mrs. Higgins went on, "a little shove. One of these stalagmites could pierce through human flesh like a knife through butter. All I would have to tell my boss would be, 'Oops! It was an accident. These crazy kids were roughhousing with each other. I tried to stop them, but you know how kids are.'"

She seemed to get excited thinking about pushing somebody onto a stalagmite.

"Or maybe I could do it over in the back corner there, where it's dark," she said. "You'd get impaled on two stalagmites, and I'd just leave you there to rot. They wouldn't find you for *years*. Eventually your

bodies would calcify and you would become part of the caverns."

She had a wistful look on her face, like she was recalling a fond memory. Then she shook her head to clear it.

"But of course, I don't do that anymore," Mrs. Higgins said. "I'm turning over a new leaf, as they say."

Pep grabbed Coke by the elbow.

"Let's blow this pop stand," she whispered, dragging her brother toward the exit.

"Hey, did you send us a cipher at the Fourth of July fireworks?" Coke asked as they were leaving.

"I don't know what you're talking about."

"Liar!"

"Bye now!" Mrs. Higgins called after them sweetly. "It was so nice to see you! Do come again! Watch your step on your way out. I don't want anyone to get *hurt*."

Then she broke into a cackling laugh.

Coke and Pep ran out of there two steps at a time.

Chapter 10

AN AMAZING COINCIDENCE

Coke and Pep came running through the Luray Caverns gift shop like they were in the Olympics, almost knocking over a rotating rack of miniature license plates with people's first names on them.

(Does anybody ever *buy* those things? Oh, never mind.)

"Don't you want to get souvenirs?" their mother asked as they dashed through. "That way you'll have something to remember this place."

"Oh, we'll remember it," Pep said. "Can we please get out of here now?"

Go to Google Maps
(http://maps.google
.com/).

Click Get Directions.

In the A box, type
Luray VA.

In the B box, type
Mount Solon VA.

Click Get Directions.

Dr. McDonald pulled out of the parking lot and found his way to Route 211 heading west. Mrs. McDonald got out of her seat and busied herself in the little RV kitchen, making sandwiches for everyone's lunch.

It was pretty country outside, but Coke and Pep didn't pay much attention to the scenery rushing by the window. Both of the twins had been freaked out by the encounter with Mrs. Higgins in the underground cave.

Maybe she was harmless now, they thought. After all, she didn't threaten them or make any move to hurt them. But still, it was hard to trust someone with her track record.

Coke turned on his iPod and bobbed his head to the music. Pep settled her mind down by pulling out her notebook and working on the message she had seen in the sky at the Fourth of July fireworks.

LEVEL VIS 1

She wrote each letter on a smaller scrap of paper and juggled the scraps around, as if they were on a

Scrabble rack. . . .

$$I \; SELL \; VIVE$$
$$LISLE \; VIVE$$
$$ILL \; VIS \; EVE$$
$$VEILS \; VEIL$$
$$LIVE \; LIVES$$

No luck. Pep was getting frustrated. It didn't usually take her this long to crack a cipher.

After about twelve miles on Route 211, Dr. McDonald merged onto a big interstate highway, I-81 heading south. Mrs. McDonald passed around her sandwiches.

"Hey kids!" she said, "guess what we're going to see this afternoon?"

"Another giant ball of twine?" guessed Coke.

"No. The National Jousting Hall of Fame!"

"Jousting?" asked Pep. "You mean, like, with horses?"

"Yup."

"That's stupid," Pep said. "Who wants to watch two idiots charge at each other on horseback with long pointy poles?"

Coke and Dr. McDonald raised their hands. Again, it's a guy thing.

They pulled off the highway at exit 240 and drove by some rolling hills and lovely Virginia farmland

until they reached the little town of Mount Solon, where the National Jousting Hall of Fame is located.

Well, to be honest, the Hall of Fame is really just one dusty room in the Natural Chimneys Regional Park visitor center. But it is for real. Go ahead and look it up if you don't believe me.

"What could they possibly have in a jousting hall of fame?" Pep asked as she opened the door.

Not much, really. Inside, there was a suit of armor,

a mannequin dressed like a medieval page, and some lances. Though disappointed, Mrs. McDonald dutifully took notes and photos for *Amazing but True*.

A little sign said that jousting demonstrations were given in the park behind the visitors' center. The McDonalds went out back and were fortunate that the demonstration was just about to begin. Two men were on horseback, covered head to toe in armor. You couldn't even see their faces. A small group of families had gathered around them.

"Jousting is one of the world's oldest sports," one of the jousters said. "Do any of you kids know anything about jousting?"

"Medieval knights would charge toward each other and try to knock the other guy off his horse," Coke said. "They were usually trying to win a fair maiden's hand."

"That's right," the second jouster said. "But today, jousting is a regular sport."

He explained that they use a series of small rings, which are suspended vertically from a metal rod. A jouster on horseback will charge eighty feet down a straight track and try to "catch" the rings at the end of his wooden lance. As jousters get better at it, the rings become smaller and harder to spear.

"Do those guys sound familiar to you?" Pep

whispered to her brother while one of the jousters showed people his lance.

"No, why?" Coke asked.

"I think I've heard their voices before."

"You're nuts."

"Jousters come from all over the world for our annual tournament," the first jouster continued. "It's getting more and more popular each year. In fact, jousting is the official sport of Maryland. Would any of you like to learn how to do it?"

"No thanks," Coke said. "We just had lunch, and my mother told me never to joust on a full stomach."

People laughed, but nobody volunteered.

"Then we'll show you how it's done," said the second jouster.

He gave the reins a snap, and his horse galloped down the road, then turned around and charged back. He was holding his lance out in front of him, and at the last second he aimed it for the ring that was suspended over the road. He speared it cleanly and got a nice round of applause.

After the jousters had repeated that a few times, they jumped off their horses and took a bow. The crowd dispersed, and the two jousters led their horses toward the stables at the far end of the field.

"Mom, can we get their autographs?" Pep asked.

"What do you want their autographs for?" she replied. "They're not famous or anything."

"Who cares?" Coke said. "They're cool. They *should* be famous."

"An autograph would make a great souvenir," Pep said. "It would give us something to remember this by."

"Okay, go ahead, if you want," said Mrs. McDonald. "Dad and I will be in the RV."

By the time the twins made it out to the stables, the two jousters had already peeled off their suits of armor. They hadn't taken off their helmets yet.

"Can we have your autographs?" Pep asked, holding out her notebook and a pen.

"Sure!"

The jousters signed Pep's notebook and handed it back to her. Then they pulled off their heavy steel helmets and replaced them with . . . bowler hats!

Coke and Pep freaked.

"It's you!" Coke shouted. "The bowler dudes!"

"At your service," said the bowler dude with a mustache.

"Run, Pep!"

I know what you're thinking, dear reader. You're thinking that the bowler dudes are going to kidnap Coke and throw him into a giant shredder they have stored in the stables. But you're wrong. Totally wrong. In fact, the twins didn't even run away. There was something about the genuine, twinkling smiles on the bowler dudes' faces that kept Coke and Pep from bolting.

"You're killers!" Coke shouted, pointing an accusing finger at both of the bowler dudes. "You tried to kill us at the singing sand dunes in Nevada! You grabbed us at The House on the Rock in Wisconsin!"

"Relax!" said the clean-shaven bowler dude. "My brother and I are out of that business."

"He's lying!" Coke told his sister. "Don't believe a word of it, Pep!"

"My brother is telling the truth," said the mustachioed bowler dude. "After Archie died and Dr. Warsaw got married, we didn't know what to do with ourselves. Mrs. Higgins became a spelunker. Then we heard about this place. It's a great way for us to blow off steam and practice our art—the art of jousting."

"That's a lotta bull," said Pep. "We're not falling for that."

"Oh, no, it's true, sweetheart," said the mustachioed bowler dude. "We're all about the rings now."

Coke peered into his eyes, as if that would enable him to see into the man's soul. The guy looked so sincere.

"You expect us to believe that it's just a *coincidence* that you're here at the same time that we're here?" Pep asked.

"The coincidence is that *you're* here at the same time that *we're* here, sweetheart," said the clean-shaven bowler dude. "Are you sure you're not following us around?"

"Yes!" Pep exclaimed.

"People *are* capable of changing, you know," said his mustachioed brother.

"Why should we trust you?" asked Coke.

"Well, look at it this way," the mustachioed bowler dude said, picking up his lance. "See this? It's seven feet long. The end is quite sharp, as you can see. Nobody's around. If I wanted to, right now I could take this lance and thrust it into your heart. You would be dead almost instantly. But I'm not doing that, am I?"

He put down the lance and straightened his tie. The twins were still not convinced.

"Did you send us a cipher at the Fourth of July fireworks?" Coke asked.

Go to Google Maps
(http://maps.google
.com/).

Click Get Directions.

In the A box, type
Mount Solon VA.

In the B box, type
Lexington VA.

Click Get Directions.

"A cipher?" both of the bowler dudes replied. "What's a cipher?"

"C'mon, Pep, let's blow this pop stand."

Chapter 11
DREAMING HAPPY DREAMS

Coke and Pep didn't know what to think anymore. After his marriage to Aunt Judy in Washington, Dr. Warsaw had vowed that he was going to get them, but there had been no attempt on their lives since then. Mrs. Higgins could have easily harmed them at Luray Caverns, but she didn't. The bowler dudes could have finished them off at the Jousting Hall of Fame but didn't lay a hand on them. Maybe Bones and Mya had been right. Maybe nobody was trying to kill them anymore.

By this time, it was late afternoon. Dr. McDonald was

determined to make it through the state of Virginia and stop for the night at a campground somewhere near the state line. He stayed on rural roads heading south out of Mount Solon until he was able to merge on I-81 and push the RV to seventy miles per hour. They were making good time. Soon they passed the exit for Lexington, Virginia.

"Hey, you'll never believe what they have in Lexington!" Mrs. McDonald said, paging through her guidebook.

"What?" everyone asked.

"Stonewall Jackson's grave!" she replied. "Not just his arm. His real gravesite!"

"You're kidding me!" Coke exclaimed. "For real?"

"Yes, and his stuffed horse, Little Sorrel, is in Lexington too," Mrs. McDonald said.

"We should go!" Pep exclaimed.

In the driver's seat, Dr. McDonald rolled his eyes. Soon it would be dark out, and the thought of driving to the next exit and finding his way back to Lexington didn't appeal to him.

Besides, a grave is a grave. To him, the location of a person's remains was not as important as the location where they lived their life, where they achieved their accomplishments.

"I wish somebody had mentioned that before we

passed the Lexington exit," he announced. "There might not be another exit for miles. I don't want to go back now."

"That's not fair, Ben!" protested Mrs. McDonald. "When we were near the gravesite of Stonewall Jackson's *arm*, you said you didn't want to go because it was just his arm. You said you'd go if it was the gravesite of his whole body! And now we get to the gravesite of his whole body and you don't want to go there either."

"But it's *not* the gravesite of his whole body," Dr. McDonald replied. "It's missing an arm."

"Ben, that's not fair!"

Coke laughed, but Pep just listened in silence, worried. Her parents had certainly been arguing a lot lately. Usually they got along pretty well. Maybe they had just been pretending all that time. Maybe being cooped up together in this RV for so long had brought out the problems in their relationship. Maybe they really didn't love each other. Maybe they were going to get a *divorce*.

A foul mood settled over the family as they drove south on I-81. Mrs. McDonald had been planning to stop off in a town called Natural Bridge to visit the Virginia Safari Park. But now she was afraid to even bring it up. She turned on the radio to break up the awkward silence.

"Next month is Elvis Month," boomed the DJ, "as we celebrate the life and remember the tragic passing of The King. But I just can't wait, so here's a little taste of Elvis right now. . . ."

"Blue Suede Shoes" blasted out of the speakers.

Pep was only half listening to the radio, but suddenly her eyebrows went up and her eyes opened wide. She reached for her pad and rifled through the pages until she found her notes on the cipher that she had been trying so hard to solve.

LEVEL VIS I

Of *course*! She fiddled with the letters for just a few moments, then wrote something down. Then she punched Coke in the shoulder and whispered in his ear, "I got it!"

"You got what?"

She showed him what she had written.

ELVIS LIVE

"LEVEL VIS I is ELVIS LIVE," she whispered excitedly. "It's so simple! I don't know why I didn't see it before."

"Yeah, but what does ELVIS LIVE mean?"

"It wasn't any secret message directed at us," Pep told him. "It was probably just an ad for some Elvis impersonator show! They must have mixed up the letters."

"But why would they put an ad for an Elvis imper-sonator show at the end of the fireworks?" Coke asked.

"Who knows? Who cares?" said Pep. "What mat-ters is that Bones and Mya were right. Nobody is trying to kill us anymore. Not Dr. Warsaw. Not the bowler dudes. Not Mrs. Higgins. And certainly not Archie Clone. It's all over. We're in the clear!"

It was nighttime when the McDonalds finally pulled into Paradise Lake and Campground just north of Danville, Virginia. They had a quick bite to eat, and then the twins got ready for bed.

They had made it almost all the way through the state of Virginia. There had been no attempts on their lives since Archie Clone had tried to drop them on the Washington Monument. For the first time in a long time, Coke and Pep felt totally secure. They slept soundly, dreaming happy dreams and looking for-ward to the rest of the summer and the rest of their carefree lives.

They had no idea that terrible, horrible, violent things were about to start happening to them. And one of them, of course, was going to involve a shredder.

Chapter 12
ESSE QUAM VIDERI!

Coke and Pep woke up on the morning of July 6 to the smell of waffles. Mrs. McDonald was attempting to make them on the barbecue grill outside the RV, which was a complete disaster. But the rest of the family had to give her an A for effort. Even bad waffles taste pretty good.

"I wonder how Aunt Judy and her new husband are doing," Mrs. McDonald said as they ate. "Maybe I should give her a call."

"They're on their honeymoon," Dr. McDonald said. "Leave them alone."

The twins didn't want to think about Dr. Warsaw.

They ran off to explore the campground, which had its own lake, with swimming, fishing, and paddle-boats. They chose badminton instead and played just long enough to remind themselves how boring badminton was. Then it was back on the road—Route 29 heading south out of Danville. Life was good. It was going to be a jam-packed day.

"What fascinating tourist attraction will we be visiting today, parental units?" Coke asked cheerfully. "I'm up for anything."

"Yeah, we don't care," his sister said. "I would even go to another museum."

"Isn't this the best vacation we ever had?" Coke added. "I'm having such a good time."

"Me too," Pep added. "Driving cross-country is way better than going to Disney World or some lame theme park."

Their parents looked at each other suspiciously. Neither could remember the last time the twins had been so cheery and full of enthusiasm about *anything*. Maybe when they were in second grade. Something *had* to be up.

"You kids seem awfully chipper today," Dr. McDonald said. "Did Mom put happy pills in your Corn Flakes?"

"We didn't even *eat* Corn Flakes today, Dad," Pep

Go to Google Maps
(http://maps.google
.com/).

Click Get Directions.

In the A box, type
Danville VA.

In the B box, type
High Point NC.

Click Get Directions.

told him, rolling her eyes. "We had waffles. You know that."

"It was just an expression."

"Corn Flakes are an expression?" Coke asked.

"We're just in a good mood," Pep said, the cheerfulness already gone from her voice. "Aren't we allowed to be in a good mood once in a while? Now you're bumming me out."

And . . . it was over. The moment had passed. Back to normal.

"That's the teenagers I know," Mrs. McDonald muttered.

The family had only been on the road for a few minutes when a sign came into view.

"Woo-hoo!" yelled Coke. *"Esse quam videri!"*

"What does that mean?" asked Pep.

"How should I know?" her brother replied. "I don't understand Latin. But it's the North Carolina state motto."

"You memorized the state motto in Latin even though you don't understand the language?" Pep asked. "That's demented."

"Don't call your brother demented," yelled Dr. McDonald from the driver's seat.

"I can't help knowing stuff," Coke explained. "I memorize *everything*."

"I wonder why states need to have a motto anyway," Mrs. McDonald said. "And why do they have them in Latin? Hardly anybody speaks Latin."

"Even Latinos don't speak Latin," Pep mused. "I wonder why they're called Latinos."

"Because they come from Latin America," Coke said.

"But why is it called Latin America if they don't speak Latin?" Pep asked.

"I have no idea," Coke told his sister. "But I do know that North Carolina is the largest producer of sweet potatoes in the country."

"Yeah, and the reason why you're such a moron is because your brain is clogged up with all that random information," offered Pep.

"Don't call your brother a moron," said Mrs. McDonald.

"That's okay, Mom," Coke said. "I can take it. She's just jealous because I'm smarter than she is."

"You are not."

"Are too."

"R2D2!"

"C3PO!"

"Hey, knock it off back there!" Dr. McDonald hollered. "I'm getting a headache."

"So where are we going today?" Coke asked. "What do they have in North Carolina?"

Mom took out her laptop and started poking keys.

"Oh, it's a wonderful state," she said. "There's so much to see. But it's very wide, and some of the places are just too far away from each other, I'm afraid. We'll have to choose a few."

"I'd love to go to search for the lost colony on Roanoke Island," said Dr. McDonald.

"What's that, Dad?" asked Pep.

"It was the first English colony in America," he replied. "This was before Plymouth. Before Jamestown. It was in the 1580s. Sir Walter Raleigh sent an expedition over, and the whole colony just vanished. Nobody knew what happened to them. When the next ship came over, the only thing left was the word *Croatoan* scratched into a tree."

"Cool," said the twins.

"So in other words, there's nothing to see there," Mrs. McDonald said dismissively. "Hmm, there's a fifteen-foot tall statue of a moose, in Mooresville, North Carolina, but that's all the way on the coast. The world's largest hammock is in Point Harbor. . . ."

Dr. McDonald gripped the steering wheel tightly.

"I'm not driving hundreds of miles to see a statue of a moose," he said.

Mrs. McDonald never looked up from her computer screen.

"You kids should find this to be quite interesting," she said. "North Carolina is famous for twins. It says here that Chang and Eng Bunker were the original Siamese twins. They were joined at the sternum and lived in Surry County. And get this—they both got married and fathered twenty-one children between them!"

"Gross!" said Pep.

"Chang and Eng died on the same day in 1874," Mrs. McDonald read, "and they're buried in White Plains, North Carolina."

"Let's go there!" Coke exclaimed.

"Then there's Billy and Benny McCrary," said Mrs. McDonald. "They were the world's *heaviest* twins— 720 and 750 pounds."

"Whoa!" Coke exclaimed.

"Which would you rather be," asked Dr. McDonald, "a conjoined twin, or a seven-hundred-pound twin?"

"I'd rather be me," Coke replied.

"Anyway, their tombstone is in Hendersonville," said Mrs. McDonald.

"Gravesites are actually pretty boring," Pep said. "You don't really see anything."

"I'm glad you feel that way," Mrs. McDonald told her, "because Dad and I already decided we're going to a *birth* site today instead."

"Birth site?" asked Coke. "Birth site of who?"

"Whom," she corrected. "We're going to Pepsi's birth site."

"Wait a minute," Pep said. "Coke and I were born in the same place, of course, and you always said we were born in California."

"Oh, we're not going to *your* birth site, honey," her father said. "Pepsi the *drink* was invented in New Bern, North Carolina. So that's where we're going today."

New Bern is more than two hundred miles to the east, and the kids would go stir crazy if they had to sit in the car that long. So Mrs. McDonald decided to break up the trip into a few "bite-sized portions."

They continued south on Route 29 for almost an hour. The highway bends to the right after Greens-boro, North Carolina, and soon after they rolled into the town of High Point. Dr. McDonald stopped the RV at the intersection of Westwood and Hamilton Streets, pulling into the largest parking spot he could find.

"Why are we stopping here?" Coke asked.

"Look across the street," said his mother.

The twins looked out the window and saw one of the most unusual buildings they had ever seen.

"Whoa!" Pep marveled. "It's a chest of drawers."

"Not only is it a chest of drawers," said her mother. "It's the world's *largest* chest of drawers!"

Sure enough, it was. Everybody piled out of the RV and crossed the street to have a closer look. It was a spectacular building, eighty feet tall.

"Why is it here?" Pep asked.

"This is High Point, North Carolina," Mrs. McDonald told them, "and it's the furniture capital of the world."

"You gotta be kidding me," Coke said. "Furniture needs a capital? They might as well have a capital of carpeting and wall coverings."

"It does look just like a chest of drawers," Dr. McDonald admitted. "And it is rather large."

"This will be great for *Amazing but True*," Mrs. McDonald said. She backed up into the street and started snapping pictures and taking notes.

And then, quite suddenly, somebody screamed, "Watch out!"

Coke looked up at the last millisecond. A very large object had fallen out of a window above. Coke did an instant mental calculation to determine that the thing was on a trajectory to land directly on his sister's head.

"Pep!" he shouted.

But she wasn't reacting quickly enough. So Coke took a running dive, wrapped his arms around his sister, and tackled her. The two tumbled to the concrete, landing with a thud.

"What the—"

Inches from Pep's head, the large object hit the sidewalk. *BOOM.* Splintered wood flew everywhere.

For a second, nobody spoke. Then, their parents rushed over.

"Are you okay?" Dr. McDonald asked Pep.

"I think so," she said.

Pep's heart was racing as she imagined what would have happened if she had been standing a few inches to the right. A crowd was starting to gather. People were taking pictures of the scene with their cellphone cameras. The police had been called.

"You saved my life!" Pep told her brother.

"I just . . . reacted," Coke said, helping Pep up off the sidewalk. "I saw something falling. What was it?"

"I think it was a chest of drawers," Mrs. McDonald said, examining a piece of wood with a knob on it at her feet.

"A chest of drawers fell out of the largest chest of drawers in the world?" asked Dr. McDonald. "That's kind of strange."

"It fell, or maybe it was *pushed*," Coke said.

"Don't be silly," Mrs. McDonald said. "Are you suggesting that somebody did that on *purpose*? Why would anyone want to hurt Pep?"

Coke and Pep looked at each other. Their parents, of course, were completely unaware of what the twins had been through on this trip so far. Since the day Coke and Pep were recruited to join The Genius Files program back in California, they had been forced to jump off a cliff, locked in a burning school, pushed into a sand pit and left to die, thrown into a vat of

Spam, zapped with electric shocks, lowered into boiling oil, drowned in ice cream, almost deafened by heavy metal rock music, and chased through the streets of Chicago by enraged Cub fans.

Coke helped his sister, still trembling, back into the RV. Their parents gave a statement to the police, who had just arrived on the scene.

"It was probably just a freak accident," Coke told his sister. "It was a coincidence that you happened to be standing on that spot at the same moment the thing fell."

"But why would a chest of drawers suddenly fall out of a building?" Pep asked. "Much less a building that's an enormous chest of drawers itself?"

"Who knows?"

"I have a bad feeling about this," Pep said.

Go to Google Maps (http://maps.google.com/).

Click Get Directions.

In the A box, type High Point NC.

In the B box, type Raleigh NC.

Click Get Directions.

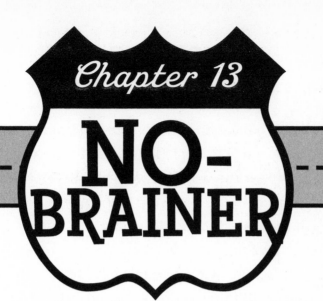

Chapter 13

NO-BRAINER

It took less than two hours on I-85 and I-40 to make it to the eastern edge of Raleigh, the capital of North Carolina. Coke whiled away the time listening to music and gazing out the window. Pep wrote postcards to her friends back in California. As the miles rolled by, the freak accident in High Point began to recede from their minds.

Dr. McDonald took exit 13A off the Raleigh Beltline toward downtown and made a left on Sunnybrook Road. From there it was a short distance to a parking lot outside a brick building with a sign out front.

POE CENTER FOR
HEALTH EDUCATION

"Health education?" Coke groaned, taking out his earbuds. "You gotta be kidding me! If you look in the dictionary for the word *boring*, I bet there's a picture of this place."

"Oh, be quiet," Mrs. McDonald told him. "You're going to love this."

Construction work was being done in the small parking lot, but finally Dr. McDonald found a spot big enough for the RV. The family had to dodge a backhoe and cherry picker to get to the front door of the Poe Center.

"Would you like to see our walk-in brain?" asked the lady behind the front desk.

"Certainly," said Mrs. McDonald. "That's why we're here." She pulled out her camera and notepad.

"Walk-in brains *are* cool," Coke admitted.

"Way cooler than brains you can't walk in," added Pep.

Behind them was an enormous floor-to-ceiling gray human-shaped head that looked like it had poked its way up through the floor from below.

"You can enter behind the ears," said the lady at the front desk.

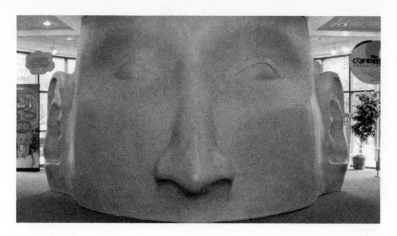

It was almost completely dark inside the big head. Then the brain started talking.

"I'm sleeping," a voice said. "I'll be with you in a second."

Suddenly two video screens flashed on where the back of the eyes would be. The McDonalds sat on benches and looked around to see sculpted red and blue blood vessels and veins running up and down the walls. They were pulsing, dimming, strobing, and changing colors. The faint sound of a heartbeat could be heard throbbing in the distance.

"Welcome to my brain," boomed a voice coming out of a hidden speaker system.

Using 3-D rendered images, the brain explained how it works, grows, learns, and needs to be protected from injury. It was educational, but not in a way that made you want to get out of there as soon as possible.

"Some reflexes are voluntary," the brain said, "while other reflexes—"

At that moment, a bunch of colored Nerf balls came shooting out of holes in the walls and flying all over the inside of the brain. The McDonald family screamed as one.

"—are involuntary."

When the short video was over, the lights came up and the McDonalds were directed to exit through the ear on the other side of the head. Mrs. McDonald jotted down some notes for *Amazing but True*.

Signs pointed to a room adjacent to the walk-in brain, where visitors could find TAM, which stands for Transparent Anatomical Mannequin.

TAM is a life-size, slowly rotating statue of a woman, one foot slightly in front of the other and her arms out as if she was taking a bow.

Oh, and you could see right through her skin. Half of TAM was muscles and blood, and the other half was bones. You could see her heart behind her ribs.

"That face is creepy," Pep said, staring. "Look at the way her eyes bulge out."

"My kidneys serve as a natural filter of my blood," TAM said through a video monitor a few feet away. "They remove wastes, which are diverted to my bladder."

TAM's kidneys lit up so the twins could see where they were located on her body. Pep touched SMALL INTESTINE on the video screen, and it lit up while TAM talked about her small intestine. In all, TAM explained fifteen of her body parts. After each one, she would smile and wink.

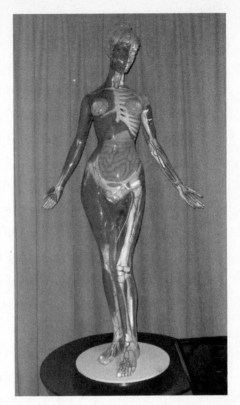

"That was cool," Coke said as they left the Poe Center.

Mrs. McDonald allowed herself a secret smile. She had just been paid the ultimate compliment by her teenage son, and she knew that if she reacted in any way, the moment would be ruined.

Next to the parking lot was a playground with a giant ear, a sliding board in the shape of a human tongue, and other apparatus involving the human body. Coke and Pep considered themselves a little too old to play in playgrounds, but there was also a rock-climbing wall, a zip line, and a heart-rate monitor to

hold their attention. Kids could run around and then place their hand on a piece of metal for ten seconds to see a digital readout of their beating heart. The twins spent about half an hour in the playground before Dr. McDonald started hinting that it was time to get back on the road.

"This place will be great for *Amazing but True*," Mrs. McDonald said as she opened the playground gate. "That walk-in brain was—"

"Watch out, Pep!" Coke suddenly shouted.

From the edge of his peripheral vision, he had spotted something falling from the cherry picker that was doing construction work in the parking lot. He gave a hard shove, sending his sister sprawling to the dirt.

"Hey! What's the big idea?" Pep shouted.

But as she turned around, she saw an irregularly shaped pink object about the size of a car smash into the blacktop at the exact spot where she had been walking. The thing must have been made of solid concrete, because when it hit the ground it cracked open and burst into thousands of pieces, which went flying all over. Everyone shielded their faces. If Coke hadn't pushed her out of the way, Pep would have been crushed.

"What was *that*?" Pep said as her parents rushed to her side.

Coke bent down and picked up a piece of the pink concrete.

"I believe that was a giant brain," he said. "I guess it was going to be part of the playground."

"Are you okay?" Dr. McDonald asked.

"I . . . think so," Pep said, still shaken up. "Coke saved my life again!"

"What are brothers for?" Coke said modestly.

"I'm going to go talk to the man operating that machine," Dr. McDonald said. "Somebody might get killed out here."

"Can we just go?" Pep said. "I don't want to talk to anybody."

"Okay, honey," Dr. McDonald said. "Anything you say."

After they piled back into the RV and were on the road, it was hard not to talk about what had just happened.

"What an odd coincidence, Pep," Mrs. McDonald noted. "When we were in High Point, you were almost crushed by a chest of drawers that fell out of a chest of drawers. And here, you were almost crushed by a giant brain right outside a building that has a giant brain."

"I'm just glad Coke saw both of them in time to push her out of the way," Dr. McDonald said. "Great work, Son!"

Go to Google Maps
(http://maps.google
.com/).

Click Get Directions.

In the A box, type
Raleigh NC.

In the B box, type
Kinston NC.

Click Get Directions.

As they got on I-40 East out of Raleigh, Pep kept trying to convince herself that the two accidents were simply random events that could have happened to anybody. Just because two freakishly coincidental things happen one after the other doesn't necessarily mean there's any connection between them.

But what if there *was*?

Chapter 14
THE KINSTON TRIO

Dr. McDonald was pushing the speed limit. It was still a long way to the Birthplace of Pepsi in New Bern. He liked driving fast, but an RV is not exactly built for speed. The dishes were rattling in the cabinets.

"Do you ever wonder where your food goes after you eat it?" Mrs. McDonald asked the twins as she passed out the tuna sandwiches she had made for lunch.

"I don't want to know," Pep said. "I'm sure it's gross."

"Well, you're going to find out," her mother told

her, "because we're going to continue on our theme of the human body. We're going to stop off and visit a giant digestive system at a hospital in Kinston."

"Yuck," Pep moaned.

"Well, it's good that we're going to a hospital," Coke remarked, "just in case something *else* falls on Pep's head."

"Very funny, jerk," said Pep as she punched him. Pep had quickly recovered from the gratitude she had been feeling for her brother after he had saved her life twice.

"Don't call your brother a jerk," said Dr. McDonald.

Kinston is a natural stopping point along Route 70 between Raleigh and New Bern. It's a small town, originally named Kingston after England's King George III. After the Revolution, the *G* was dropped in hopes that people would forget about the king. Go ahead and look it up if you don't believe me.

Dr. McDonald pulled off the highway, and it was only a few blocks to the Lenoir Memorial Hospital Health & Science Museum. The McDonalds piled out of the RV. Or I should say, *most of* the McDonalds piled out of the RV.

"Let's go, Pep," called Mrs. McDonald. "I think you're really going to like this."

"You guys go ahead," Pep replied. "I'll stay here."

"Don't be silly," said her father. "We do things as a family."

Slowly, reluctantly, Pep emerged from the safety of the RV. She looked up in the air and around her nervously, convinced that an enormous intestine was going to fall out of the sky and on her head at any moment. There was nothing dangling above that could do her harm.

As advertised, the hospital had a room with a replica of a digestive system that visitors could go through. The whole family entered through the mouth—naturally—and had to get down on their hands and knees to crawl through the throat, esophagus, stomach, and intestines. Along the way, they activated sensors that triggered audio descriptions of the functions of various parts of the digestive system. At the end, well, they crawled out the exit.

They didn't spend a lot of time at the hospital, which also featured a crawl-through model of a blood vessel, a planetarium, and other exhibits. Pep was on her guard the whole time, still convinced that something else would fall on her head.

As they walked back to the RV, Pep was cautiously looking up in the sky when—

"Watch out!" Coke yelled.

Pep hadn't noticed, but directly in front of her was

a pit, camouflaged by a thin layer of leaves. She tumbled into it with a shriek, landing on her face.

"Ahhhhhhhhhhhhhhhh!"

The pit was about six feet deep and appeared to have been constructed like a trap that would be used by a survivalist to catch animals. Fortunately there were no pointed sticks poking up from the bottom.

"Get me outta here!" Pep yelled.

"Are you okay?" Dr. McDonald asked as he helped Pep climb out of the hole.

"I think so."

"Why is there a hole in the ground here?" Mrs. McDonald complained. "It serves no purpose."

"They should at least put a sheet of plywood over this," Dr. McDonald said. "Somebody could get hurt, and the hospital would have a big lawsuit on their hands. Maybe we should go back and issue a formal complaint."

"Forget about it, Dad," Pep said. "Let's just blow this pop stand."

She seemed to be okay, except for the humiliation that comes from falling into a hole. Coke stifled a laugh, and Pep slapped him.

"This isn't funny!" she whispered to him. "Somebody's out to get me. It's probably Mrs. Higgins or those bowler dudes."

"You're just paranoid," Coke said. "All you did was fall into a hole."

"I fell into a hole after a chest of drawers and a giant brain fell on me," Pep told him. "Three things like that don't just happen to *anybody*. Those weren't coincidences."

Go to Google Maps (http://maps.google .com/).

Click Get Directions.

In the A box, type Kinston NC.

In the B box, type New Bern NC.

Click Get Directions.

107

Chapter 15

PEPSI WORLD

The McDonalds only had to drive about forty minutes on Route 70 heading west to reach New Bern, the second-oldest city in North Carolina. At the mouth of the Neuse River, it's just miles from the Atlantic Ocean.

"Hey, y'know what else is in New Bern?" asked Mrs. McDonald as she leafed through her guidebook. "The stuffed head of the horse that used to pull the town fire truck. His name was Firehouse Fred. We could go see him afterward."

"Do we have to?" Pep asked. "I don't want to look at

some dead stuffed horse's head."

Dr. McDonald pulled off the highway at the New Bern exit, made a right on Pollock Street, and drove less than a mile, taking a right on Middle Street.

And there it was—an unassuming little corner store with a blue awning. Just down the street, there

was an open parking spot big enough for the RV.

"So *this* is where Pepsi was invented?" Pep asked. There was a plaque on the wall. As she got closer, she could read the words . . .

This building marks the site of Bradham's Pharmacy where Caleb D. Bradham created Pepsi-Cola in 1898.

"Pharmacy?" Pep said.

"Back in those days," her brother told her, "pharmacies had soda fountains in them, and the pharmacist would mix up his own drinks. So this guy named Caleb Bradham began experimenting, and he hit on a formula of carbonated water, sugar, kola nut extract, vanilla, pepsin, and rare oils. In the beginning, he called the stuff 'Brad's Drink.'"

"How can you possibly know all that?" Pep asked her brother.

"I just *do*, okay?" he replied. "Bradham renamed the stuff Pepsi-Cola in 1903 after the two main ingredients, pepsin and kola nuts."

"Who cares?" Pep said, refusing to be impressed by her brother's encyclopedic knowledge of useless information.

The McDonalds went inside. The Birthplace of Pepsi was empty, or at least it was empty when it came to people. It was filled, however, with just about every Pepsi product in existence. There were Pepsi teddy bears, baseball caps, clocks, cookie jars, and earrings. Pepsi salt and pepper shakers, key chains, umbrellas, coffee mugs, and mouse pads. Pepsi zipper pulls, belt buckles, and T-shirts that read FRIENDS DON'T LET FRIENDS DRINK COKE.

"This place is just a store that sells Pepsi stuff," said Coke. "It's not like it's a museum or anything."

"It's just a big commercial for Pepsi." Dr. McDonald scoffed. "It's like all these tourist traps."

"Well, what did you expect?" Mrs. McDonald asked. "The Louvre? You're not going to find the Mona Lisa at a place like this."

"I don't even *like* Pepsi," said Coke, who always insisted that Coca-Cola tasted better than Pepsi-Cola. "I say we blow this pop stand."

"I want to look around a little," said Pep. "We came so far to get here."

"I'll be in the RV," muttered Dr. McDonald.

"Me too," said Coke.

Mrs. McDonald snapped a few photos and picked up a brochure.

"Come on out when you're finished, honey," she told Pep. "Don't listen to those boys. You take your time in here."

Now Pep was alone. She didn't even see anybody behind the cash register. She wandered around the

111

aisles, looking at the Pepsi hooded sweatshirts, the Pepsi bottle Christmas tree ornaments, the earrings made out of Pepsi bottle caps. It was a Pepsi *world*!

Growing up, Pep had always felt a little left out when she'd go into stores with her friends. Girls with names like Melissa and Ashley and Rachel could always find personalized souvenirs with their names on them. There was never anything for kids who had an unusual name. But here, everything in the store had Pep's name on it. It was almost like the whole place was devoted to her. She was mesmerized.

"Don't be sad, little lady."

The husky voice came from behind her. Pep, taken by surprise, wheeled around to see . . . Elvis Presley.

Well, an Elvis Presley *impersonator*, anyway.

There he was, in all his Elvis glory, decked out in a white spandex jumpsuit, a ridiculously wide macramé belt with metal studs, a white scarf, and a red velvet cape with elaborate embroidered designs all over it. This guy wasn't just some casual fake Elvis. He was a *real* fake Elvis. He even wore an Elvis mask, which completely covered his face.

"Do you work here?" Pep asked innocently.

"You might say that, darlin'."

He was even putting on a fake Elvis voice.

"Why are you dressed up like Elvis Presley?" Pep asked.

"Today is Elvis Day at the Birthplace of Pepsi," Elvis replied. "The King loved Pepsi. Say, are you here all by yourself, young lady?"

"The rest of my family got bored," Pep told him, "so they're waiting in the RV. But my name is Pepsi, so this place is pretty cool to me."

"You look like you've had a tough day," Elvis said in his obviously fake Elvis voice.

"Yeah," Pep said, "a chest of drawers and a giant brain nearly fell on me. And then, while I was looking up in the air for the next thing to fall on me, I fell into a hole."

"Too bad," Elvis said. "Maybe Elvis can make it . . . EVEN WORSE!"

"But . . ."

Elvis grabbed Pep roughly by the elbow, then picked her up and carried her to the back room of the store.

"Help! Let me go! Get your hands off me!"

There was a set of creaky wooden steps. Elvis dragged her down them, into a dingy basement with nothing in it but a chair, a metal tub, an old refrigerator, and one lightbulb hanging from a wire.

"Let me out!" Pep screamed. "Help! Anybody!"

"Scream all you want," Elvis said as he got a rope and began to tie Pep to the chair. "Get it out of your system. You'll feel better."

"What are you doing?" Pep begged. "Who are you? Why are you doing this to me? Are you the one who dropped the chest of drawers and the giant brain on my head?"

"Don't be silly," Elvis said. "The King would never do something like that. I *pay* people to do those things for me."

"Why? What did I ever do to *you*?" Pep yelled, struggling against the ropes.

"You ask too many questions, for one thing," Elvis told her. "You're starting to get on my nerves. Things will be a lot better once you're *dead*."

"Dead?" Pep gulped. "Why me? Stop! Let me go! Who are you? Are you working with Dr. Warsaw?"

The ropes were tight. Pep wasn't going anywhere. Elvis pulled the metal tub over and jammed Pep's feet into it.

"I guess you didn't get the message I sent you," he said.

"What message?"

"Remember the fireworks on the Fourth of July in Washington?" Elvis said. "Remember the message at the end?"

"The cipher?" Pep asked. "I saw it. LEVEL VIS I. I figured it out. ELVIS LIVE."

"No, you dope!" Elvis said with a laugh. "I thought

you were such a smart cookie. You got it *completely* wrong."

"Well, if the message didn't say ELVIS LIVE, what did it say?"

Elvis looked at her and laughed again.

"EVIL ELVIS," he said.

Chapter 16

IT'S NOW OR NEVER

Evil Elvis?

Of *course*! The letters didn't spell LIVE. They spelled EVIL! EVIL is LIVE backward! Pep would have kicked herself, if she had been able to get her legs free. How could she have been so dumb?

She tried to peer under the Elvis mask while he leaned over to take her sneakers off. He was humming the Elvis song "Don't Be Cruel." Pep tried to kick him, but her feet were tied tightly against the chair.

"What are you going to do to me?"

"What does it *look* like I'm going to do to you?" Elvis said. "I'm going to kill you."

"What about my brother?"

"I'll take care of him after I finish *you* off," Elvis told her. "Killing two kids at once isn't nearly as much fun. I want to do it one at a time so I can really savor each murder. You only die twice, ha-ha-ha-ha!"

Evil Elvis was insane, clearly. The voice sounded familiar, but Pep couldn't place it.

Satisfied that his victim was secure, Elvis pulled a cigarette lighter out of his pocket and flicked it on. He waved it around Pep's face, letting the flame linger near her nose for just an instant so Pep would feel the heat.

Here he was, taunting her with fire, and he had sent that message at the fireworks show. Pep made a mental note that Evil Elvis was a pyromaniac. If she was ever able to get out of this, she would at least be able to tell the police something about him.

"You're going to *burn* me?" Pep asked, sobbing. "Is that how you're going to do it?"

"Oh no, that would be cruel," Elvis said. "I have a better idea."

He went to the refrigerator and pulled open the door. Pep could see that it was filled with two-liter bottles of Pepsi. Elvis twisted off the cap from one of them and began to pour the contents into the metal tub that held Pep's feet. When that bottle was empty, he opened another one and poured that in. Then he

poured a third bottle in. Pep's feet were covered in soda.

"What are you doing?" Pep shouted.

"Do you know what Pepsi is made of, Pepsi?" he asked.

"High fructose corn syrup?" she replied.

"Yes, and phosphoric acid," said Evil Elvis gleefully. "It's right on the label. And do you know what phosphoric acid does to the human body?"

"Quenches our thirst?" Pep said, still squirming to try and get free.

"Cute," Elvis said. "Soda and sweets rot your teeth, right? Well, did you ever put a tooth into a glass full of soda and let it sit there overnight? In the morning, there's nothing left! The tooth dissolved. The acid will eat away at your feet until there's nothing left but bone."

"You're crazy!" shouted Pep.

"If the phosphoric acid in Pepsi will do that much damage to a little tooth," Elvis continued, "just imagine what it will do to human flesh. How ironic. Pepsi will be killed by Pepsi!"

As if to confirm his insanity, Elvis let out a cackling laugh.

"You monster!" Pep shouted at him. "Help! Help! *Somebody!*"

Elvis took the white scarf from around his neck and wrapped it around Pep's mouth.

"Quiet," he instructed her. "Your pathetic cries for somebody to rescue you are annoying, do you know that?"

"Mmphf!" Pep shouted.

"It won't be long," Elvis said cheerfully. "Can you feel the acid starting to eat away at your toes?"

Pep did feel a burning sensation. She tried to call to her mother and father, but the sound was muffled by the gag in her mouth.

"Oh, don't worry," Elvis assured her. "This won't be a burden to your family. After the phosphoric acid eats away at your flesh for twenty-four hours, the blood will drain out and there won't be much left. I'll make an anonymous call to the morgue in the morning so they can send somebody over to dispose of your bones."

"Help!"

"*Tomorrow . . . will be too late,*" Elvis began to sing. "*It's now or never. My love won't wait.*"

"Let me go!"

"Sorry, can't help you there, darlin'. Elvis has left the building."

And with that, he ran up the stairs and out the door, cackling the whole time.

Chapter 17
THE CALLING CARD

Back in the RV, Coke and his parents were starting to get impatient. Dr. McDonald looked at his watch.

"What's taking her so long?" he said. "I thought she was just going to buy herself a souvenir and that would be it."

"Women and shopping, Dad," Coke said. "You know."

"That's a sexist comment!" said Mrs. McDonald. "How about a little patience? I had to sit and wait for *you* while you were watching that ball game in Chicago."

"She's probably buying up the whole store and wasting money," said Dr. McDonald. "I read an article about this somewhere. People with unusual names love to buy things that have their name on it. It validates them. I *told* you we should have named her Ashley."

"You wanted to name her Sprite," said Mrs. McDonald. "One of us should go check on her."

"I'll do it," sighed Coke.

Coke hopped out of the RV and jogged down the street to the Birthplace of Pepsi. It was empty, just as it had been the first time he went in.

"Pep! You in here?"

No answer. Coke looked all around and, seeing no sign of his sister, pushed open the door leading to the back room. It was a small office, also empty. He stopped. Was that a muffled sound coming from below the floor? He found the steps and rushed downstairs.

That's where he found his sister, bound and gagged, her feet submerged in a tub of some dark liquid, desperately trying to yell for help.

"Pep!" he shouted, taking the scarf off her mouth. "What are you doing here?"

"Oh, I came down here and tied myself to this chair for the *fun* of it!" she yelled at him. "You dope! I was kidnapped!"

"Hey, don't yell at *me*," he replied. "I'm rescuing you."

"Get me outta here!" she shouted. "Quick, before the acid eats through my flesh!"

"I'm working as fast as I can," he said, trying to untangle the ropes around her feet. "Who did this to you?"

"Evil Elvis," she told him. "That's what the cipher meant. I was wrong. It wasn't ELVIS LIVE. It was EVIL ELVIS. He's an Elvis impersonator. He's the one who dropped the chest of drawers and the giant brain on me."

"What was an Elvis impersonator doing in the Birthplace of Pepsi?" Coke asked.

"Trying to kill me!" Pep shouted. "He stuck my feet in the tub of Pepsi so it will eat at my flesh. Hurry up! I think the bone in my leg is about to come through the skin!"

Coke stopped. Then he started laughing.

"What's so funny?" Pep asked. "Stop laughing at me!"

"You think dipping your feet in soda is going to make your flesh dissolve?" Coke asked, doing his best to avoid doubling over.

"It won't?" Pep said meekly.

"That's one of those urban legends, you dope!"

Coke told her. "Soda can't do that."

"It can't?"

"Of course not," Coke said as he removed the last of the rope that was binding her. "That's one of those stories that gets passed around on the internet so much that people think it's true. It's a hoax. There's more acid in orange juice than in Pepsi. See for yourself. Your feet are fine."

Pep pulled her feet out of the tub and counted her toes. Satisfied that all ten were still there, she wiped them on Coke's shirt and put her sneakers back on.

"Why would Evil Elvis do this?" she asked her brother. "He could have killed me easily enough if he wanted to."

"This is his calling card," Coke guessed. "He wants us to know he's out there, watching us. He's trying to get into our heads. Mind games, you know. And he's probably nuts, like those other people who have been chasing us."

"He told me he's going to get *you* after he takes care of me," Pep told her brother.

"Oh yeah?" Coke said. "Not if I get him first. And he's gonna have to do more than stick my feet in a tub of soda pop."

They ran out of the Birthplace of Pepsi and back down the street to the RV.

"So what did you buy?" Dr. McDonald asked Pep as he started up the engine.

"Nothing."

"All that time and you didn't buy *anything*?" said Mrs. McDonald. "What were you doing in there? We were starting to get nervous."

"Not to worry, Mom," Coke explained. "Pep got kidnapped by an evil Elvis impersonator who tied her to a chair and said he was going to soak her feet in Pepsi until it ate away at her flesh."

"Kids . . . ," muttered Dr. McDonald, shaking his head.

Chapter 18

A SENSELESS ATTACK

It was getting late, and everybody was hungry. Just down the block from the Birthplace of Pepsi was Captain Ratty's Seafood and Steakhouse. The McDonalds decided to splurge on a rare sit-down dinner. The grown-ups took their time eating and really enjoyed the meal.

By the time the family was finished, it was close to nine o'clock and nobody wanted to start out on another long drive. Fortunately, the Moonlight Lake RV Park was also in New Bern, right across the bridge. Mrs. McDonald checked in at the office while the twins gathered some sticks to start a campfire.

Pep hadn't done much talking during dinner, and her brother could see that she was still visibly nervous and upset about what had happened in the basement of the Birthplace of Pepsi. The twins had just been getting used to the idea that they were safe from danger, and now they realized how wrong they were. Somebody was out to get them, again. It wasn't Archie Clone. He was dead. Mrs. Higgins was working at Luray Caverns. The bowler dudes were into jousting. Dr. Warsaw was away on his honeymoon with Aunt Judy. Now they had another nemesis.

Evil Elvis.

"Don't worry," Coke told his sister. "I'll protect you. Remember, I'm Ace Fist."

He did his spinning karate kick. Pep appreciated the support, but it didn't give her much comfort. What would her brother be able to do to protect her? With crazy people like Evil Elvis running around loose, a thirteen-year-old brown belt is only so much help.

The twins gathered a load of wood, and their father used it to build a nice little fire. Mrs. McDonald had come back from the campground office with some marshmallows, graham crackers, and Hershey bars. It wasn't long before the whole family was sitting around the fire making s'mores.

"So how do you kids like North Carolina so far?" asked Dr. McDonald.

"It's great, Dad," Coke said.

"We love it," said Pep.

In fact, the drive through North Carolina had been a *horrible* experience, at least for Pep. A chest of drawers had been dropped on her in High Point. A giant brain had almost brained her in Raleigh. She had fallen into a hidden hole in the ground in Kinston. And then, of course, there was the encounter with Evil Elvis at the Birthplace of Pepsi.

She couldn't *wait* to get out of North Carolina.

It was July 7. In the morning, Pep did a little fishing in the pond near the RV, but her heart wasn't in it and she didn't catch anything. She couldn't shake the sense of impending doom that had taken over her. It was a relief when they got on the road again, heading west on Route 70. It would be a three-hour drive to the South Carolina border.

Coke thought it would be a good time to take

Go to Google Maps (http://maps.google.com/).

Click Get Directions.

In the A box, type New Bern NC.

In the B box, type Rose Hill NC.

Click Get Directions.

inventory of what he and Pep had in their backpacks. They emptied them out on the seat between them. A jar of bubbles. A can of Spam. A couple of yo-yos. A can of Silly String. A Frisbee. Some other miscellaneous stuff they had picked up at gift shops along the way.

"How are we supposed to defend ourselves against Evil Elvis with *this* junk?" Coke whispered to his sister. "We need to get some *real* weapons, and we need to get them soon."

"How are we going to get real weapons?" Pep asked. "Don't you have to be eighteen or twenty-one or something?"

"How should I know?"

"You know every other stupid thing in the world," Pep told her brother. "It would be nice if you actually knew something that mattered."

"Shut up."

"*You* shut up."

"Knock it off back there!"

Dr. McDonald turned onto Route 11 South, and then onto an even smaller road, Highway 117, which eventually becomes North Sycamore Street in Rose Hill, North Carolina. The first thing you see when you enter the town is this sign. . . .

"You gotta be kidding me," Coke said.

Dr. McDonald pulled over and parked the RV.

"This seems like a good place to stretch our legs," said Mrs. McDonald, grabbing her camera.

"It is *not*!" Coke complained. "You know we're only stopping here because you want to see that frying pan."

"Frying pan?" asked Mrs. McDonald. "I don't know what you're talking about."

They walked across Sycamore and turned left on Main Street. That's where Mrs. McDonald stopped.

"Wow! Drink it in, you guys!" she announced. "You don't see something like *this* every day."

And there it was, inside a large red pavilion.

"It's . . . a big frying pan," Pep said, unimpressed.

"Amazing!" gushed Mrs. McDonald. "Simply amazing."

"What do they cook in this thing?" Coke asked. "Giant eggs?"

Mrs. McDonald started taking notes and snapping photos for *Amazing but True.* Dr. McDonald sighed, then sat down on a bench to read the newspaper.

The frying pan, Coke had to admit, was pretty awesome. It even smelled like a frying pan, or at least one that hadn't been washed very well. But then, how would you wash a frying pan the size of a small swimming pool?

Coke and Pep were walking around the perimeter of the frying pan when Coke noticed a figure standing at the far corner of the pavilion. He was wearing a sparkling white jumpsuit and a ridiculously wide belt.

"It's him!" Coke said. "Evil Elvis! I'm gonna kill him!"

Coke took off like he'd been shot from a gun. It only took five steps until he was full speed, and then he took a running leap to jump on Elvis's back from behind. Taken completely by surprise, Elvis fell forward, landing in a pile of dirt next to the enormous frying pan. Coke was still on the guy's back, and he began furiously punching him from behind.

"Don't you *ever* bother my sister again!" he shouted. "You hear me?"

"What?!" the Elvis impersonator protested, his face full of dirt as he tried to cover his head and fend off the blows coming at him. "What are you talking about? Who *are* you?"

Coke was still flailing at the man with both fists. He knocked off the Elvis wig and kept right on punching the man's bald head.

"If you so much as touch my sister or any member of my family—"

Pep came running over, followed by her parents and a few curious onlookers. Dr. McDonald grabbed Coke around his waist and just about *tore* him off the man's back. Pep shook her head sadly and mouthed the words "That's not him" to her brother.

"Are you crazy?" Dr. McDonald said as he flung Coke to the ground. "Leave that man alone!"

The Elvis impersonator was still on the ground, stunned. There was dirt all over his white jumpsuit and a trickle of blood dripping from his upper lip.

"What were you thinking?" Mrs. McDonald asked Coke.

"He's . . . Elvis . . . ," Coke stammered, not really knowing how else to explain his actions.

"You are grounded, young man!" Dr. McDonald shouted. "I don't want to hear another word from you."

Pep pulled her brother aside while their parents went to help the Elvis impersonator.

"Are you crazy?" Pep asked. "What did you do *that* for?"

"I was trying to defend you!" Coke said. "I thought he was Evil Elvis."

"There are *lots* of Elvis impersonators," Pep told

him. "They're not all evil!"

"It was an impulse," Coke admitted. "I saw him, and I went nuts."

"Just calm down, okay?" his sister advised him. "And apologize to that man."

Coke and Pep came back to the "scene of the crime." Their mother was holding a tissue up to the man's face and helping him adjust his wig.

"I'm really sorry, sir," Coke said. "I just went a little crazy for a minute."

"You *should* be sorry!" his mother said.

"Hey, it's all good," the Elvis impersonator said. "Stuff happens."

"Here," Dr. McDonald said, handing the man a twenty-dollar bill. "I want you to have this, with our apologies. It should cover your cleaning bill, at least."

"So what brings you here?" Mrs. McDonald asked the man as she brushed the dirt off his jumpsuit.

"I'm on my way to a convention of Elvis impersonators in Memphis," he replied. "But this is sort of a hobby of mine. I'm into big frying pans."

"That's an odd thing to have as a hobby," said Dr. McDonald. "So you came here just to see the largest frying pan in the world?"

"Don't judge the man, dear," Mrs. McDonald said. "Different strokes for different folks, right?"

"Actually, there are *six* frying pans that people claim are the largest," Elvis said. "I'm proud to say I have visited them all."

"This guy has *way* too much time on his hands," Coke whispered to his sister.

Mrs. McDonald was fascinated, taking a notepad out of her pocket to write down some quotes.

"You may find it interesting to know that this frying pan holds two hundred gallons of oil and uses forty gas burners," Elvis explained. "It can cook three hundred sixty-five chickens at a time. That would be one for each day of the year."

Mrs. McDonald was writing down every word.

"Why would anyone cook a chicken and not eat it for a year?" Coke asked.

Elvis looked at Coke for a moment, not sure if he was joking or not. Then he decided just to ignore the remark and avoid another confrontation with the boy.

"One could argue that the oversized frying pan in Brandon, Iowa, is actually the biggest," Elvis said, "because it's fourteen feet in diameter and weighs over a thousand pounds. That's significantly larger than the frying pan they have in Long Beach, Washington, which is less than ten feet, and the one in Wilmington, Delaware, which only weighs six hundred fifty pounds. It all depends on your definition of the word *largest*, of course."

"This guy is nuttier than Mom," Coke whispered.

"And of course, there's a big frying pan in Pittsfield, Maine," Elvis continued. "That one is only five feet in diameter, but it's coated with Teflon, so it's definitely the largest *nonstick* frying pan in the world. And then there's the one in London, Kentucky—"

"We really have to go," Dr. McDonald said, "but it was really nice chatting with you, and again, I'm sorry about my son."

The McDonalds hightailed it out of there before Elvis could tell them any more about the frying pan in Kentucky.

"I feel like going back there and beating that guy up *again*," Coke said as they got in the RV. "Nobody should know that much about oversized frying pans."

Go to Google Maps (http://maps.google.com).

Click Get Directions.

In the A box, type Rose Hill NC.

In the B box, type Dillon SC.

Click Get Directions.

Chapter 19

SOUTH OF THE BORDER

Regular-sized things aren't all that interesting, if the truth be known. There's nothing particularly captivating about a *normal* frying pan, or a plain old chest of drawers. But a *gigantic* frying pan, or an *enormous* chest of drawers, or a twelve-foot-tall ball of twine is inherently fascinating.

A teeny-tiny frying pan or a miniature chest of drawers would also be interesting, if such things actually existed. But they don't, outside of dollhouses. It's extremely *big* things that command our attention. There's something fascinating about them. Towns actually compete with each other and argue over which one has the largest *whatever* in the world.

Why is that?

While you ponder the question, dear reader, the McDonald family is not waiting around for the answer. They're on the move, chugging along at sixty miles per hour on Highway 117 South before exiting onto Route 41.

"Listen to this," Mrs. McDonald said as she read from her guidebook. "North Carolina not only has the largest frying pan and chest of drawers in the world. It also has the largest tire, the largest lighthouse, the largest hammock, the largest Ten Commandments, the largest sea hawk, and the largest strawberry!"

"That's really interesting, Mom," Coke lied.

"Who cares what's the biggest *anything* in the world?" Dr. McDonald asked, just looking for trouble. "It's not important."

"I care, Ben!" Mrs. McDonald replied, giving him one of those looks. "And my readers care."

That was the end of the discussion.

Coke took out his cell phone so he could send a message to his sister without his parents listening in.

U THINK MOM IS INSANE? he texted.

Just OCD Pep texted back.

It was beautiful country in southern North Carolina. They passed by Bay Tree Lake and Bladen Lakes State

Forest. When they reached the town of Lumberton, Dr. McDonald merged onto I-95, the superhighway that extends all the way from Maine down to Florida. That's when they started seeing these billboards at the side of the road.

You Never Sausage A Place—
20 MILES TO SOUTH OF THE BORDER

Everybody Needs A Little Stuff—
15 MILES TO SOUTH OF THE BORDER

World's #1 Miniature Golf—
10 MILES TO SOUTH OF THE BORDER

It was one after the other. The signs were unrelenting. The farther south they drove, the more frequently these billboards popped up.

"What does South of the Border mean?" Pep finally asked.

"Oh, you'll see," her mother replied.

Soon another sign appeared in the distance.

"Woo-hoo!" Coke hollered. "The Palmetto State!"

"Oh, and I suppose *you* know what a palmetto is?" asked Pep.

"Of course I do," Coke replied. "A palmetto is a type of palm tree. During the Revolutionary War, the British attacked a fort here that was made of palmetto trees. The fort didn't fall, so South Carolina became known as the Palmetto State."

"I hate you," Pep said disgustedly. One of these days, she decided, she would find some obscure fact her brother didn't know.

"Don't say you hate your brother," said Dr. McDonald.

"Did you know," Coke informed the family, "that in South Carolina it's illegal to keep a horse in a bathtub? That's a fact."

"Oh, just shut up already," said Pep.

The terrain was very flat, so even before the McDonalds had crossed the state line, they were able to see something very curious several miles in front of them. It was a tower, maybe two hundred feet high. As they got closer, they

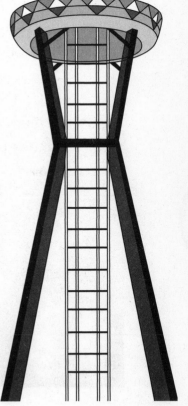

could see that perched on the top of it was, for some reason, a gigantic sombrero.

"It looks like the Eiffel Tower," Pep marveled after they had pulled off the exit, "with a Mexican theme."

"What *is* this place?" Coke asked, craning his neck to look all around.

"It's the cheesiest, schlockiest, tackiest tourist trap in the world," replied Dr. McDonald as he pulled into the immortal roadside attraction called South of the Border.

"Let's go!" shouted the twins.

Dr. McDonald thought of all the years he had spent in

school, studying to become a respected historian. And now *this*. He sighed as he drove the RV between the legs of a huge figure of a mustachioed man named Pedro, who was also wearing a sombrero and holding a big South of the Border sign.

The McDonalds drove a big loop around SOB, as it's called, and the whole family was wide-eyed.

None of them had ever seen *anything* like this place. In addition to the usual hotels, souvenir stores, and gas stations, South of the Border has six restaurants (including Pedro's Ice Cream Fiesta). It has its own amusement park (Pedroland), a wedding chapel, and a golf course (The Golf of Mexico). The whole thing is like a small, fake Mexican town, spread out over a square mile. It even has its own police and fire department. Scattered around are giant pink flamingos and silly statues of monkeys wearing T-shirts.

"Is this heaven?" asked Coke.

"No," his mother replied, "it's South Carolina."

Everything, it seemed, was neon yellow or pink. It was almost as if South of the Border wasn't sure if it wanted to be a theme park or a truck stop, and it compromised somewhere in the middle.

Dr. McDonald found the on-site RV campground (Camp Pedro, of course) and pulled in. Mrs. McDonald was excited and eager to explore the whole place. It was just perfect for *Amazing but True*.

"You kids go have fun," she instructed as she checked her cell phone for the time. "Let's meet back here at six o'clock for dinner."

Pep looked at her brother nervously. Whenever they were separated from their parents, it seemed, something bad would happen. She wanted to stick

close to her mom and dad, but at the same time she didn't want to look like a baby.

"I'll take care of her," Coke said as he put on his backpack.

"What do you need that for?" Dr. McDonald asked.

"It's my security blanket," Coke replied.

"Fill it with souvenirs," suggested his mother as she reached into her purse and gave them some money.

"You kids be careful," Dr. McDonald said before they parted company. "There are always a few creeps running around a place like this."

"We're always careful, Dad," said Coke.

One thing you can say about South of the Border—there's no shortage of souvenirs for sale. The twins didn't have to look more than five minutes before they found a store that was stuffed to the rafters with them.

This place had everything: coffee mugs, snow globes, buttons, postcards, glow-in-the-dark knick-knacks, hundreds of T-shirts, and bumper stickers. There were *eight* different kinds of back scratchers! They had serving trays, salt and pepper shakers, and bobblehead Pedro statues. Every cheesy gewgaw and doodad ever invented, it seemed, was right there.

"Hey, check it out," Pep shouted. "They have alligator repellent! You never know when *this* might come in handy."

"Look," Coke said. He was holding up a pair of underwear with the words WORLD'S LARGEST SOURCE OF NATURAL GAS on the back. "I gotta buy this."

After making their purchases, the twins strolled around until they came to the observation tower with the sombrero on top that they had seen from the highway. They went over to get a closer look, and when they got about ten feet from the bottom of the tower, Pep stopped. These letters were written in yellow chalk on the ground . . .

OLLP FK

Coke stopped too. There were no other letters written anywhere on the ground.

"What's that?" he asked. "Do you think it's—"

"—a cipher," Pep said, finishing his sentence for him. "It's definitely a cipher."

"What does it mean?" Coke asked, not even bothering to try to figure it out himself. He just wasn't good at the stuff.

"Give me a minute."

Pep stared at the letters intently. The cipher was shorter than others she had seen, so she figured it shouldn't be very hard to crack. She jumbled the

letters around in her mind, but that didn't yield many words. It had to be some kind of a substitution cipher, in which one letter substitutes for another. But what were the substitutes?

She imagined the alphabet in her mind, as if it was written across the whiteboard at school. What if everything was moved one letter to the right? So A was really B, and B was really C, and—

No, that wouldn't work. And it also wouldn't work if everything was moved *two* letters to the right.

"It might be a reverse alphabet cipher," Pep said. "In that case, A becomes Z, B becomes Y, C becomes X, and so on."

Coke took a sheet of paper out of his backpack and wrote out the alphabet. Then he wrote out a reverse alphabet below it . . .

ABCDEFGHIJKLMNOPQRSTUVWXYZ
ZYXWVUTSRQPONMLKJIHGFEDCBA

They looked at the letters on the ground again: OLLP FK.

"If this is right, the letter O is an L," Pep said.

"Then the two Ls would be Os," said Coke.

"The P has to be a K," Pep said, "which means the first word is L-O-O-K."

"And the second word is—"

Before Coke could finish deciphering FK, Pep

looked up and saw something falling from the top of the sombrero tower. It was coming down right over their heads!

"Coke, watch out!" she screamed, slamming her body against his with enough force to knock him over.

The falling object was a large black garbage bag. It hit the spot where Coke had been standing with so much force that it burst apart, littering the ground with hundreds of what appeared to be small gold trophies. A lot of them were broken on impact. The distant sound of an evil, cackling laugh could be heard.

"You saved my life!" Coke said, still in a daze. "If you hadn't figured out the cipher so fast, that stuff would have landed on my head."

"What are sisters for?"

Pep bent down and picked up one of the trophies. In fact, they were statues—souvenir replicas of the observation tower they had fallen from, and made from razor-sharp plastic. If one of these things landed on your head, you wouldn't be getting back up anytime soon. Pep looked at her brother.

"It's Evil Elvis, or one of his flunkies," she said. "He dropped the chest of drawers on me from that giant chest of drawers in North Carolina, and he dropped that brain on me when we were at the walk-in brain.

Now he's dropping little observation towers out of the observation tower, and he's aiming for *you*."

"I'm gonna kill him!" Coke said, jumping to his feet. "Let's go!"

He ran over to the observation tower and started charging up the steps.

"Wait! Stop!" Pep yelled after her brother. "What if you're wrong, like you were when you attacked that guy at the frying pan?"

"I'm gonna kill him!" Coke repeated. There was no stopping him.

Pep ran and followed her brother up the steps. The tower was higher than either of them realized, and by the time they got up to the top, they were both gasping for breath.

"Where is he?" Coke asked, looking around with a wild look in his eyes. "I'm gonna kill him!"

But for better or worse, the observation deck at the top of the tower was completely empty. Evil Elvis, or *whoever* had been up there, was gone. Maybe he had parachuted off while the twins were climbing the steps. Maybe a helicopter had come and scooped him off the top of the tower. There was no way of knowing.

The giant sombrero covered the top of the tower and served as a great scenic lookout. After their breathing returned to normal, Coke and Pep walked all the way around the brim, looking down to see if they could spot Evil Elvis. There were hundreds of people below walking around South of the Border, but none of them was wearing a white jumpsuit.

After five minutes, they gave up and just looked at the scenery. From this high vantage point, they could see all of South of the Border. That's when Coke spotted this sign . . .

BOOM POW!
THE FIREWORKS SUPERSTORE

He looked at it for a moment, and slowly a smile spread over his face.

"Are you thinking what I'm thinking?" he asked.

"That depends on what you're thinking."

"I'm thinking we buy some fireworks," Coke said.

"Are you crazy?"

"Look," Coke said to his sister, "you know as well as I do that Evil Elvis is trying to kill us. We both agreed that we need some weapons to defend ourselves. Mya and Bones said they won't give us any, so we have to get them on our own. And there they are, waiting for us to take them away!"

"Fireworks are *dangerous*!" Pep protested. "Every year I see stories on the news about kids getting hurt

because some fireworks blew their finger off or took their eye out."

"Well, of *course* fireworks are dangerous!" Coke said. "That's why we need 'em! If they weren't dangerous, they wouldn't do us any good, right? We need to show this Evil Elvis creep who he's dealing with. Come on!"

Coke started charging down the stairs of the observation tower, almost as quickly as he had charged up them a few minutes earlier. Pep, lacking any better plan, followed him.

"I don't feel good about this," she said.

Chapter 20
BANG FOR YOUR BUCK

"**L**et me do the talking, okay?" Coke told his sister as they approached the front of Boom Pow! The Fireworks Superstore.

"Okay, okay."

Before they opened the door, Coke took out his wallet to see how much money he had. Minus the five dollars he had spent on gag underwear at the souvenir store, there were fifty dollars he had saved from raking leaves back home, plus the money his mother had given him.

"Do you have any money?" he asked Pep.

"I have forty dollars," she replied. "But that's the money Mom gave me plus all my babysitting money. I don't want to spend it all on fireworks."

"Look," Coke said, "Evil Elvis is trying to kill us. Do you grasp the magnitude of that? He's trying to *kill* us. *He's* got weapons. You know what they say. Desperate times call for desperate measures. We need all the firepower we can afford."

"Okay, okay," Pep said, handing over the money she had worked so hard to earn.

There were big signs plastered all over the window of the store.

Call us before your next party or special event!

Get more bang for your buck!

Come here for all your pyro needs!

Coke pulled open the door. The place was huge. It looked a little bit like a supermarket, but instead of aisles marked SOUP, DAIRY, and FROZEN FOOD, they were marked MISSILES, ROCKETS, AERIAL REPEATERS, and ROMAN CANDLES. The twins picked an aisle randomly to walk down. It was jammed with all kinds of explosives in scary-looking packages, with names like Midnight Dynamite, Purple Powerhouse, Nuclear Warhead, Sky Slammer, Freaky Tiki, and Hairy Eyeball.

"This isn't a store," Pep marveled. "It's an arsenal."

"If this place ever catches on fire," Coke said, "I just hope I'm here to watch it blow."

A tall, skinny, and extremely well-pimpled employee wearing a Boom Pow! T-shirt came toward them. He looked like a high school kid. His name tag said Trey.

"I'm sorry, but you gotta be eighteen years old to buy fireworks, y'know," Trey told them. "You two don't look eighteen."

"Let me handle this," Coke whispered to his sister. "This redneck looks pretty dumb. He's probably the result of some serious inbreeding."

Coke straightened his posture to address the kid.

"You're right, technically," he said, "but we're dizygotic twins. So two fertilized eggs were implanted in our mother's uterus wall at the same time. In other words, together we're twenty-six years old."

Coke glanced at Pep to make sure she wasn't going to open her big fat mouth. Trey stared at the two of them for a moment, looking back and forth from one to the other.

"Okay," he finally said. "What do you need?"

"We figured we'd buy some firecrackers," Pep said.

"Firecrackers?!" Trey spit on the floor, then hollered, "Hey, guys, get this! These kids want to buy *firecrackers*!"

A few men standing around the cash register started falling all over themselves like it was the funniest thing they had ever heard.

"I thought we agreed that *I* would do the talking?" Coke whispered to his sister angrily. Then he put one arm on Trey's shoulder and said, "She's just kidding. We want the *real* stuff."

"Well, now you're talkin'," Trey said. "We got megabangers, herbies, California candles, Texas rockets, Killer Comets, triple-whistler bottle rockets, anything you want. The X-18 Mega Blast is on sale this week. How much money are you thinkin' to spend?"

"We have a hundred bucks and change," Coke said. "Maybe you can make some recommendations?"

"Hmmmm," Trey said, picking up a large box from a shelf. "Lemme see. We just got in these American Beauties. They're five-hundred-gram cakes that explode in red, white, and blue with white strobes. Or maybe you'd rather go with a Barrel Buster. The blast opens up like a round of machine-gun fire. It's *awesome*."

"Which one makes the biggest explosion?" Coke asked.

"Well," Trey said, "both of 'em are pretty intense. I mean, you get too close to either of these babies, and you'll have a headache that'll last you a lifetime. But if you're looking for flat-out, blow-out-the-ears power, I'm thinking the best thing for you might be our Classic Repeater Four Pack. Four repeaters in one package—Green Bamboo, Big Snow, Yellow Bees, and Cloud Dragon."

"Wow, you sure know a lot about fireworks," Coke said.

"Yeah," Trey replied. "I'm sorta into blowing stuff up."

"Who isn't?" said Coke.

"I'm not," said Pep.

"Well, you're a girl," Trey said with a laugh. Then he and Coke high-fived each other.

"You can do some serious damage with this stuff," Coke said.

"You ain't kiddin', buster," Trey agreed. "It's like having a missile silo in your own backyard. Listen, you look like good kids. I'll tell you what I'm gonna do. For a hundred bucks, you can have the Classic Repeater Four Pack, and I'll throw in an Exploding Mosquito for free. It has the maximum powder content allowed for helicopters."

"Cool!" said Coke. "Thanks!"

"Don't mention it," Trey said. "And because the

Fourth of July is over and we're trying to get rid of inventory, you can also have a Silver Stunner. It includes a free fiberglass launching tube."

"Wow!"

"And just so you know," Trey continued, "everything we sell comes with a one hundred percent no-dud guarantee. We stand behind our products. But *you* shouldn't stand behind our products. Ha-ha-ha! That's a little fireworks joke there. You see, if you stand behind our products, you might get your head blown off."

"We get it," Pep said, unamused.

Trey walked the twins to the cash register and rang up their purchases.

"Do you need any racks or tubes?" he asked. "Artillery shells?"

"No thanks, we're good," Coke said, stuffing the explosives into his backpack. "It was a pleasure doing business with you."

"Have a nice day, and thank you for shopping at Boom Pow!"

After they left the fireworks store, Coke and Pep stopped off at a place called Reptile Lagoon that had all kinds of snakes, crocodiles, alligators, and turtles. They spent about an hour there looking at all the reptiles. By the time they were finished, it was close to six o'clock. When they got back to the RV, their parents were cooking hot dogs and hamburgers on the outdoor grill. Coke ditched the backpack full of fireworks discreetly behind his seat.

"Isn't this place great?" asked Mrs. McDonald excitedly. "Did you kids buy any good souvenirs? What did you get?"

"I bought a can of alligator repellent," Pep said.

"I got a pair of underwear that says WORLD'S LARGEST SOURCE OF NATURAL GAS," said Coke.

"That's not funny," his mother said disapprovingly.

"Hey, *you're* the one who bought the POUPON U toilet seat!" Coke said.

The gag toilet seat Mrs. McDonald had bought at the Mustard Museum in Wisconsin was still sitting in the back of the RV.

"He's got you there, dear," said Dr. McDonald.

The burgers and dogs were excellent, and after dinner the whole family took a walk to the other end of South of the Border for ice cream and a round of miniature golf. By the ninth hole, Coke had nearly forgotten that just a few hours earlier, someone at the top of the observation deck had dropped a bag full of observation-deck statues on top of him.

When they got back to the RV, it was dark outside. Mrs. McDonald went to update *Amazing but True* while Dr. McDonald checked on the barbecue pit. There were still a few red-hot embers in there, so he carefully placed some sticks on top and blew on them to make the fire come to life again.

"Hey, kids, c'mere," he said. "I want to tell you a story. Like in the old days."

Coke rolled his eyes. When they were little, their father would come in their room at night, sit down on the floor, put an arm around each twin, and tell them stories. Sometimes it was a fable he remembered from his own childhood. Other times he would just make something up as he went along. It was nice.

But the twins were thirteen now. It seemed a little babyish to still be listening to your dad tell you a bedtime story. But the twins sat on the wooden bench next to the fire and cuddled with their father anyway, for old times' sake.

"Did I ever tell you the story of Blackbeard the pirate?" he asked them.

"We saw the movie, Dad," Pep said. "Johnny Depp was in it."

"Not *that* story," Dr. McDonald said softly. "It happened not far from here, off the Carolina coast. He was born in 1680, and his real name was Edward

Teach. But everyone called him Blackbeard."

"I guess he had a black beard, huh, Dad?" asked Coke.

"Yeah, I guess so. And he tied colored ribbons to it. He wore a big black hat and a big black coat."

"Even during the summer?" Pep asked. "It must have been really hot—"

"Shhhh," her father said. "This is a true story. Under the coat, Blackbeard would hide a sword, some knives, and two pistols. He would look for trading vessels along the coast that were transporting valuable cargo. Then he'd board them and rob them. If somebody put up a fight, he'd kill them."

"What a jerk," said Pep.

"Oh, Blackbeard was a *bad* guy," her father continued. "He attacked and pillaged ships along the Carolina coast starting around 1717. And then one day they got him. The governor of Virginia sighted Blackbeard's ship, and the governor ordered his crew to hide belowdecks. When Blackbeard boarded the ship, the crew attacked him. For all the heartache he had caused so many people, they stabbed him twenty times and they shot him five times. After all of that, he *still* wasn't dead, so they hanged him."

"That's the story?" asked Coke. He seemed to remember that the stories his dad used to tell had

happy endings, and there were usually furry animals and candy involved.

"No, that's only part of the story," Dr. McDonald said, almost whispering now. "Here's the thing. After they stabbed, shot, and hanged Blackbeard, they chopped off his head and put it on a stick for everyone to see. Then they threw his body into the ocean."

"This story is getting gross, Dad," said Pep.

"What happened next?" asked Coke.

"Well, according to local legend," Dr. McDonald told the twins, "the body didn't sink into the water like everybody expected. Instead, Blackbeard's head on a stick started shrieking, and his headless body swam around the ship."

"Without a *head*?" asked Pep.

"Yup. And it swam around the ship *seven* times!"

Pep felt the hairs on her arm go up.

"Not only that," Dr. McDonald continued, "but to this day, a lot of locals around here claim to have seen Blackbeard's headless body floating on the waves and giving off a mysterious phosphorescent glow. Some people say they've seen it rise out of the water with a lantern and walk ashore to search for its head. His ghost leaves no footprints, so we don't know where it is. He could be out here right now. That's the story of

Blackbeard the pirate."

"Oh, great," Pep said, "and you expect me to go to *sleep* after hearing that?"

"I'll protect you," Coke said as they went inside the RV to brush their teeth and get ready for bed.

Pep had a hard time falling asleep that night. She was lying on her back thinking about Blackbeard when suddenly she bolted upright.

"Do you hear something?" she asked Coke, shaking him to wake him up.

"Huh? It's just Blackbeard's headless body looking for its head," Coke told her. "Go back to bed."

"I hear music," Pep said.

"You're hallucinating."

But it wasn't Blackbeard's body walking around in the middle of the night looking for its head. It was

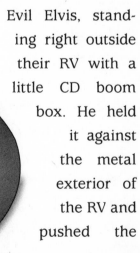

Evil Elvis, standing right outside their RV with a little CD boom box. He held it against the metal exterior of the RV and pushed the

play button.

"Don't Be Cruel" came out of the speakers. For the rest of the night, Coke and Pep would not be able to get those words out of their heads.

Go to Google Maps (http://maps.google .com).

Click Get Directions.

In the A box, type Dillon SC.

In the B box, type Columbia SC.

Click Get Directions.

Chapter 21

A GIFT

When Pep woke up the next morning, the first thing she did was to go outside and look for signs of anything suspicious. Sure enough, taped to the exterior of the RV right near her window was an envelope. Pep ripped it open and found a slip of paper with this written on it . . .

OGO THT LEV INI RGO OM

"I knew it!" she said as she ran inside to show it to her brother.

"What does it mean?" Coke asked.

"I don't know," Pep replied, "yet."

The family got a late start that day because Mrs. McDonald did a load of laundry in the campground washing machine and Coke did a dump to clear out the RV holding tank. Finally, around ten o'clock, they left South of the Border and were on I-95 South again. A billboard said PEDRO SAD THAT YOU ARE LEAVING.

Dr. McDonald hoped to make it halfway across South Carolina, to Columbia, before lunchtime. It would be a little more than a hundred miles.

As usual, Mrs. McDonald had her head in a guide-book.

"We could stop off at the Rice Museum in George-town," she mused out loud.

"*Please* tell me the Rice Museum is named after somebody named Rice," said Coke. "Jerry Rice, the football player? Condoleezza Rice?"

"Actually, no, it's a museum *about* rice," said Mrs. McDonald.

"No!" the kids shouted.

"They *can't* have a museum about rice!" Coke whined. "It can't be true!"

It *was* true, but much to the relief of Coke and Pep, their mother did not insist on visiting the Rice Museum.

Pep took out her notebook and examined the cipher that had been taped to the RV in the middle of the night: OGO THT LEV INI RGO OM. Coke opened his backpack and read over the instructions that came with the fireworks he had bought.

When I-95 intersected with Route 20 near Florence, South Carolina, Dr. McDonald pulled off the road and into a service station. It was one of those big ones, with a dozen pumps and a convenience store.

"We need to gas up," he announced.

"Why didn't you gas up when we were at South of the Border?" Mrs. McDonald asked him. "There was a gas station there."

"I forgot, okay?" he replied. "I'm not perfect."

"Are you and Mom fighting?" Pep asked from the backseat.

"No!"

Dr. McDonald inserted his credit card into the slot on the pump to pay for the gas.

CARD DENIED flashed on the little screen as the credit card popped back out.

"What?!"

"Is there a problem, dear?" asked Mrs. McDonald.

"The stupid machine won't take my credit card," he replied.

He tried again, and again the card was denied. Mrs. McDonald hopped out and went to see if she could

help. An attendant saw that they were having trouble and came over.

"There must be some mistake," Mrs. McDonald told the guy. "We used this credit card just this morning, and it was fine."

"Take it into the office," said the attendant. "They'll take care of you."

Dr. and Mrs. McDonald walked purposefully to the office, around the back of the gas station. Most people don't carry around a lot of cash in their wallets. To a grown-up, a credit card is sort of like a life preserver. If they lose it, or can't use it, they're sunk—especially if they're far from home.

Coke and Pep went back to what they were doing. But suddenly, the front doors opened and two grown-ups got in. It wasn't their parents. It was Bones and Mya.

"Bones!" shouted Pep.

"Mya!" shouted Coke. "What are *you* doing here?"

"We realized we were wrong," Bones said. "We told you that you were safe, that you didn't have to worry anymore."

"Your lives are in serious danger," said Mya. "Someone is trying to kill you."

"Gee, ya think?" Pep said sarcastically.

"Yeah," Coke said, "we kinda figured it out when

my sister had a chest of drawers dropped on her head and she was kidnapped by an Elvis impersonator."

"Where were *you*?" Pep said, her voice rising in anger. "I thought you were going to help us. You never do *anything* for us!"

"I'm sorry," Bones said sincerely. "We've let you down. But we came here today to make it up to you."

"We brought a present," Mya said, reaching into her bag.

"What is it?" Coke asked. "Another bottle of bubbles? Some more bars of hotel soap? Thanks for *nothing*."

"You've been asking us to give you a weapon," Mya said, "and we didn't want to because you're so young. But we thought it over. And now that we've seen the way you've handled yourselves, we think you're ready."

Coke threw a look at Pep, shaking his head to tell her not to let Bones and Mya know about the arsenal of weapons they had purchased at the fireworks store.

Mya pulled a blue Frisbee out of her bag and handed it to Pep.

"You're giving us a Frisbee?" Coke asked. "Oh, gee, *thanks*!"

"It's not just *any* Frisbee," Bones told him. "It's a Frisbee *grenade*."

"For *real*?"

"This is just like the one you used in Washington to blow up Archie Clone's helicopter," Mya explained. "It's only a little heavier than a regular Frisbee, but it's packed with sophisticated electronics and plastic explosives. This is the on/off switch here, on the inside of the lip."

"Wow," Pep said, cradling the Frisbee grenade in her arms like a baby.

"You've earned it," Bones said.

"There are just two things I need to tell you about the Frisbee grenade," Mya told Pep. "First of all, it can't get wet. If it hits any water, it won't work. Got that?"

"Yeah," Pep said.

"The second thing is, it detonates upon the *second* impact. So if you want to blow something up, you have to skip the Frisbee off the ground first, or have it ricochet off something. Do you know how to skip it?"

"Sure," Pep said, making a mental note.

"One more thing," Bones said. "This thing cost fifty thousand dollars. So be *very* careful with it. It's not for playing catch. It's not for target practice, and it's not for fun. It's for defending yourselves if your lives are being threatened. You get just one shot with this thing. So make it count."

"I will," Pep vowed.

"Thanks, you guys," Coke said. "This really means a lot to us. But you better get out of here. Our parents will be back any second."

"Don't worry about them," Mya said. "There's nothing wrong with your father's credit card. We arranged for it to be denied so they would have to go to the office for a few minutes. As soon as we give the signal, your parents will be told everything is fine with the credit card."

"Clever," Coke said.

"Hey, before you go," Pep said, pulling out the slip of paper with the latest cipher on it, "do you have any idea what this means?"

OGO THT LEV INI RGO OM

Bones and Mya looked at it but could not decipher the message. They gave each of the twins a hug and said good-bye. A minute later, Dr. and Mrs. McDonald returned to the RV.

"Is everything okay?" Coke asked.

"Yeah," his father replied. "It was just some dumb mistake with the credit card company. Are you kids okay?"

"Couldn't be better," Coke replied.

It was true. Even though Dr. Warsaw was still alive,

Mrs. Higgins couldn't be trusted, the bowler dudes were psychotic, and Evil Elvis was out there determined to get them, Coke was feeling pretty good. If anybody tried to mess with him or his sister, they would be in for a big surprise. He and his sister had enough firepower to take out a small tank.

Now they were armed, as they say, to the teeth.

Chapter 22

ACCIDENTS HAPPEN

You're probably getting a little impatient, maybe even a little angry, by now. On the first page of this book, you were told—you were *promised*—that Coke was going to be thrown into a giant shredder. So far, we have encountered no shredder. Not a *shred* of a shredder. You have every right to be mad. Promises should be kept. But trust me, dear reader. Your patience will be rewarded. Soon.

Interstate 20 starts close to the gas station where the twins met up with Bones and Mya. It cuts all the way across the state of South Carolina and doesn't end until it reaches West Texas.

The highway looked like it stretched ahead to infinity, so Pep pulled out the cipher she had been puzzling over ever since she received it that morning.

OGO THT LEV INI RGO OM

It looked so easy, but she couldn't seem to crack it.

Then, as they were driving through Lee State Park near Bishopville, South Carolina, she figured it out. Pep noticed that when the first four letters— OGOT—were reversed, it spelled out TOGO. TOGO very probably meant TO GO, which possibly meant GO TO. "Go to" would be an obvious way to start a message.

So if reversing the first two letters made sense, and reversing the next pair of letters made sense, what would happen if she reversed *all* the pairs of letters after that? She wrote it out in her notebook. . . .

GOT OTH ELI VIN GRO OM

"Go to the living room!" Pep shouted.

"What are you talking about?" her father said from the driver's seat. "It's an RV. We don't even *have* a living room."

"Uh, nothing, Dad," Pep said. "I was just having a dream or something."

She leaned over to show Coke how she had figured out the cipher.

"Go to the living room?" Coke whispered. "What's that supposed to mean?"

"Beats me."

As the highway unrolled endlessly in front of them, each person in the family was deep in thought. Pep tried to figure out what "go to the living room" meant. Coke was trying to figure out how he would be able to use the fireworks he had purchased as weapons without hurting anyone in his family. Mrs. McDonald was trying to think of a way to convince the rest of the family to visit the Button Museum, which was right nearby.

Yes, it's a museum about buttons. Look it up if you don't believe me.

And Dr. McDonald was thinking about his next book. He had to admit that the last one he had written, *The Impact of Coal on the Industrial Revolution*, had been a bomb. Oh, it sold a few thousand copies and received some nice reviews in scholarly journals. But hardly anybody had read it. He wanted to write something that *millions* of people would read. Working as a university professor was rewarding, but what he *really* wanted was to see his name on the best-seller list.

"I was thinking that I should try something more commercial next time," he announced to nobody in particular. "I should write a biography of somebody *really* famous."

"I thought you had already decided that you were going to write a biography of Herbert Hoover, dear," said Mrs. McDonald.

He *was* going to write a biography of President Hoover. But that was before they visited the Hoover Historical Center in North Canton, Ohio, and found out it was the home of the guy who owned the Hoover Vacuum Cleaner Company.

"I changed my mind," he replied. "Nobody cares about Herbert Hoover. Even *I* don't care about Herbert Hoover."

Soon they started seeing road signs for Columbia,

the capital of South Carolina. Stomachs had started rumbling. It would be a good time to stop for lunch. Mrs. McDonald decided not to mention the Button Museum to the rest of the family. She had another idea.

"Take exit 73A, Ben," she said. "It's coming up on the right."

"What's there?" he asked.

"Trust me."

She directed him into the heart of the city, until they reached Taylor Street. He pulled into the parking lot of the AgFirst Farm Credit Bank.

And there it was, right in the middle of the parking lot.

"Behold!" announced Mrs. McDonald with a sweep of her arm.

"What is it?" asked Pep.

"What do you *think* it is?" said her mother. "It's the largest fire hydrant in the world!"

"You gotta be kidding me," said Coke.

But Coke's mother wasn't kidding. Oh sure, there's a twenty-five-foot fire hydrant

in Beaumont, Texas, and a twenty-nine-foot fire hydrant in Elm Creek, Manitoba. But this one was *thirty-nine feet* tall and made of five tons of steel set in a concrete base. Even Dr. McDonald was impressed by the sheer grandeur of it.

"Why do they have an enormous fire hydrant in the middle of this parking lot?" asked Pep.

"They must have some really big fires around here," Dr. McDonald remarked.

"Or some really big dogs," said Coke.

Mrs. McDonald was awestruck and rushed to take photos and jot down notes for *Amazing but True*.

"Now I want to show you something even *more* interesting," she said, stepping out of the RV. "Follow me."

Coke grabbed his backpack and Pep took her Frisbee grenade. They had decided to bring their weapons with them wherever they went, just in case.

"You don't need that stuff," Mrs. McDonald told them. "We're just going up the street."

"I want to take it, Mom," said Coke.

"You heard your mother," said Dr. McDonald. "Leave that stuff here."

Reluctantly the twins left their weapons in the RV and walked around the corner to the other side of the parking lot.

"Behold!" announced Mrs. McDonald with another sweep of her arm.

"What is it?" asked Coke.

"It's Tunnelvision!"

What else could you call it? Painted on the wall of the Federal Land Bank Building was a spectacular mural depicting a tunnel that had been cut through mountain rock, with the highway curving through it and into distant hills toward a brilliant orange sunset. The mural, which is fifty feet high and seventy-five feet across, fills the wall of the building. It's so realistic, they say, that birds will sometimes fly into it. The McDonalds stood in wonder.

"Cool!"

"Amazing!"

"Incredible!"

"Awesome!"

"And who would think," said Mrs. McDonald, "that two such amazing things would be a block away from each other. That's why I wanted to come to Columbia."

She moved back so she could take photos of Tunnelvision. Coke and Pep went up to touch the wall, just to make sure it wasn't a real tunnel.

"It's such a great optical illusion," Coke said. "I feel like I could walk right through the mural, just like on those old Road Runner cartoons."

At that moment, at the other end of the parking lot, a light blue Ford Escort was revving its engine. It shifted into drive, started rolling forward, and began picking up speed. It was heading straight toward the wall.

The car got up to forty miles per hour before anybody noticed that it was going *awfully* fast to be in a parking lot. It wasn't until it reached fifty miles per hour that anybody noticed it was heading straight for Tunnelvision.

"Coke, watch out!" Pep screamed as she grabbed her brother's arm and yanked him out of the way mere milliseconds before the car slammed into the wall at the exact spot where he had been touching it.

Booooooooooooooooooom!

The impact caused the front end of the Ford to crumple like a cheap accordion. It collapsed into itself in such a way that the driver's seat was compressed to a few inches. Smoke poured out of what used to be the engine. Fragments of the former windshield flew in all directions. A siren sounded in the distance almost immediately.

"You saved my life again!" Coke said to his sister as they lay on the asphalt a few feet from the smoldering wreck.

Their parents came running over. Strangers came running over too, some to offer help and others just to gawk. In less than a minute, a police car and ambulance had arrived on the scene.

"You okay, son?" asked one of the cops as Coke got up and brushed himself off. "Anything broken?"

"No, I don't think so," he replied, his heartbeat still well above normal. "It missed me by a few inches."

"You're a very lucky young man," the cop told Coke. "One more second, and you would be dead right now."

"That's the third time it happened this year," said the cop's partner. "This mural is just *too* realistic. It's a public hazard, I say."

"We better go see how the driver made out," said the first cop. "This ain't gonna be pretty."

They ran around to the other side of the smoking car to pull the driver out. The car had been crushed so badly that you couldn't even see the driver from the outside.

"Nobody could survive that," one of the cops said, grabbing his walkie-talkie. "Better call the morgue."

You never want to see another human being die, especially in such a tragic manner. But the twins were willing to make an exception in this case. Secretly Coke and Pep hoped the driver was Evil Elvis. Or Mrs. Higgins. Or one of the bowler dudes. Or maybe even Dr. Warsaw himself. If those creeps were out of the picture, it would be the end of their problems. But when the cop managed to stick his head into the driver's-side window, he found something even *more* surprising.

"There's nobody in the car," he said.

"What?" said his partner. "That's impossible."

"It must be remote controlled," said the first cop. "Y'know, one of those new high-tech cars that drive themselves."

"I'll be darned. Never seen anything like *that* before."

"Do this job long enough, you'll see everything."

Mrs. McDonald peered inside the car for herself, just to be sure the policemen were right.

"Why would somebody drive a remote-control car into a wall?" she asked.

"I guess they didn't think it was a wall," said one of the cops. "They thought it was a tunnel."

Coke and Pep didn't mention to the police that whoever was controlling that car knew full well that they were driving it straight into a wall, and that they drove it straight into the wall *specifically* because Coke was standing in front of the wall. Nobody would ever believe that.

A tow truck arrived to haul the crumpled car away, and gradually the curious onlookers left. The police wrote out a report and told the McDonalds they could go.

"You kids certainly are accident-prone lately," Mrs. McDonald said. "One day a chest of drawers nearly falls on Pep's head, and the next day a remote-control car almost slams into Coke."

"Yeah," Pep said weakly. "Those were pretty amazing coincidences."

As they walked back to the RV, Coke had a look on his face, a look of steely resolve.

"Do you think it was Evil Elvis?" his sister asked him.

Go to Google Maps (http://maps.google.com).

Click Get Directions.

In the A box, type Columbia SC.

In the B box, type Travelers Rest SC.

Click Get Directions.

"Oh, I'm *sure* it was Evil Elvis," Coke replied. "I'm gonna get him for this."

The McDonalds stopped off at a nearby Subway for lunch, and then got on I-26 West out of Columbia, which cuts right through Sumter National Forest. Mrs. McDonald was searching in her guidebook and on her laptop for a campground somewhere near the Georgia border.

"Can we stay somewhere that has a swimming pool?" asked Coke.

"Yeah, we never get to go swimming," Pep said.

Most of the campgrounds Mrs. McDonald found were located in state parks or next to lakes, and they didn't usually have swimming pools.

"This place looks nice," she said, showing them a photo in the guidebook. "It says here they have a babbling brook that runs the length of the campground."

"We don't care about brooks," said Coke, "babbling or otherwise."

"They have a well-manicured nature trail," Mrs. McDonald pointed out.

"We don't care about nature trails," said Pep.

"You kids are tough to please," their mother said. "They have a horseshoe pit . . . a volleyball court . . . pool table . . . propane station . . ."

"We don't care," the twins said as one.

". . . and they have a swimming pool!" Mrs. McDonald shouted. "Yes! They have a swimming pool!"

"Yeah!"

"It's a few minutes from Greenville, nestled in the foothills of the Blue Ridge Mountains," said Mrs. McDonald. "It says here that 'You will feel so relaxed and removed from the hustle and bustle of everyday life.'"

"Oh, please *please* can we go there?" Pep begged.

Dr. McDonald took I-385 up past Greenville and the Poinsett Highway past Furman University into the small town of Travelers Rest. It wasn't hard to find Valley Park Resort. It was exactly as it had been advertised—babbling brook, shady trees, beautiful mountains.

"Can we go swimming?" the kids asked almost as soon as the RV pulled into the parking lot.

"Go!" Mrs. McDonald enouraged them. "Swim! Have fun!"

The twins quickly changed into their bathing suits and followed the signs to the pool. It wasn't exactly

Olympic-sized, but it would do. A sign at the edge of the pool read

WARNING
NO LIFEGUARD ON DUTY

SWIM AT YOUR OWN RISK

"Geronimo!" Coke shouted as he cannonballed into the deep end. Pep carefully waded in at the other end. They met in the middle of the pool.

After the automobile "accident" at Tunnelvision, the twins thought that taking a swim would calm their nerves. And it did. After a fierce splash fight, Coke and Pep rolled over and floated on their backs, looking up at the sky. There's something about being surrounded by water that makes a person feel safe. Maybe it reminds us of what life was like in the womb.

And yet, at the same time, it was hard for Coke and Pep to get Evil Elvis out of their heads. He was a different kind of criminal. Like a cat that likes to play with its prey, it seemed like Evil Elvis enjoyed toying with them. Why else would he put Pep's feet in soda and tell her it would eat away at her flesh? Why else would he hide outside their RV in the middle of the night playing Elvis music? Why else would he dig a giant pit in the ground for Pep to fall into? He could have killed them anytime he wanted to, but he seemed to enjoy taunting them. And he seemed to have an unlimited amount of time and money to do it.

The twins, of course, finally had some weapons they could use to defend themselves. But they still had a big disadvantage. They didn't know where or when Evil Elvis was going to strike. How do you get back at somebody if you can't find him?

These are the kinds of thoughts that were buzzing around in the twins' minds as they relaxed in the pool. After floating on his back for a long time, Coke rolled over to do a dead man's float. And when he opened his eyes and looked under the water, this is what he saw, written, in large red letters, on the bottom of the pool.

MOOVRETTHTOGO

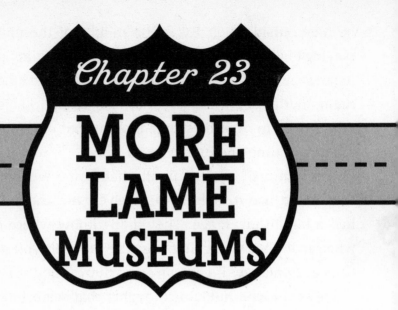

Chapter 23

MORE LAME MUSEUMS

"Oh no, not *another* one!" Coke said underwater, the bubbles pouring out of his mouth.

MOOVRETTHTOGO. What could *that* possibly mean?

Coke showed his sister the letters at the bottom of the pool and quickly memorized them. As soon as they climbed out of the water and toweled off, Pep wrote the cipher down on a blank page in her notebook and got to work.

MOOVRETTHTOGO. She figured that before anything else, she would try out the same strategy that had worked on the last cipher. She reversed the first two letters, and then reversed the third and fourth letters.

OM OV. OMOV

Well, that didn't mean anything. This would require a bit more thought. Pep resolved to work on it more seriously later.

If they hadn't decided to go swimming, it occurred to Coke, they would have never seen the message left for them at the bottom of the pool. How was it, he wondered, that Evil Elvis was able to send them these messages so easily? He had to know exactly where they were going to go and when they were going to be there. Then he had to get to that location first, plant the cipher, and leave.

Coke scratched his head and remembered . . . the computer chip. Way back in California, when they had first joined The Genius Files program, GPS devices had been implanted into both of their scalps. Their every move could be tracked. And there was no way to remove the computer chips. How Evil Elvis managed to write letters on the bottom of a pool filled with water was anybody's guess.

"We've got to tell Mom and Dad what's going on," Pep told her brother as they headed back to the RV. "Honesty is the best policy."

Go to Google Maps
(http://maps.google
.com/).

Click Get Directions.

In the A box, type
Travelers Rest SC.

In the B box, type
Hartwell GA.

Click Get Directions.

"Don't you remember what Dr. Warsaw told us after the wedding?" Coke replied. "He said if we say one word about any of this to our parents, he'll kill them both."

"Oh yeah."

Despite everything that had happened in South Carolina, the twins somehow managed to have a relaxing dinner and get a good night's sleep. In the morning, the McDonalds pulled out of Valley Park Resort around nine o'clock and made their way to I-85 South.

The Blue Ridge Mountains appeared hazily in the distance. It wasn't long before the McDonalds started to see a lot of water out the windows on both sides, as well as people fishing, boating, and water skiing. It was enormous Lake Hartwell, which has 962 miles of shoreline. The lake was named after Nancy Hart, a woman who almost singlehandedly captured six British soldiers in the Revolutionary War.

They were going over a long bridge when a sign came into view. . . .

"Woo-hoo!" Coke shouted. "The Goober State!"

"Why are peanuts called goobers, anyway?" Mrs. McDonald asked, figuring one of them might know the answer.

"It's one of those mysteries of life," replied Dr. McDonald, "like what happened to Amelia Earhart. Hey, maybe I should write a biography about *her*."

"Actually," Coke said, "the word *goober* was an African term that was brought to America by slaves before the Civil War."

"Thank you, Mr. Know-It-All," said Pep, rubbing her eyes.

"Aren't you going to regale us with some obscure trivia about the state of Georgia, honey?" asked his mother.

Coke had to search his memory for a moment before he was able to come up with anything.

"Georgia is the nation's number one producer of the three Ps," he finally said, recalling a copy of the *Weekly Reader* from second grade. "Peanuts, pecans, and peaches."

"Everybody knows that, bonehead," Pep said with a snort.

"Don't call your brother a bonehead."

"Oh yeah?" Coke replied. "Well, the Georgia state seashell is the knobbed whelk."

"That's more like it, Son!" said his father.

Pep rolled her eyes in disgust.

By the age of thirteen, many kids take an active interest in where they go on a family vacation and even help their parents plan out the trip. But Coke and Pep were still pretty much content to let their parents take care of these details. Mrs. McDonald, in particular, seemed to really enjoy doing the research by herself and setting the agenda.

"What do they have in Georgia?" Pep asked.

"Yeah, where are we going today?" asked Coke.

"Oh, it's a secret," Mrs. McDonald told them. "We're going someplace very special to one of you. You'll find out when we get there."

"SLM," Coke mumbled under his breath to his sister. Like a lot of twins, they had developed a shorthand way of communicating information they wanted to keep private. SLM stood for Some Lame Museum.

It was just as well that Coke and Pep *didn't* know where they were going. With those computer chips implanted in their scalps, if they were to mention any location, they could be tracked more easily.

"I *will* tell you where we're *not* going," said Mrs. McDonald, looking through her guidebook. "The world's largest peanut monument, in Ashburn, Georgia. It's too far out of our way."

"Bummer," Coke said. "I really want to see that."

"The Lunchbox Museum in Columbus has more than two thousand metal lunchboxes and seventeen hundred thermoses," said Mrs. McDonald. "That could be very interesting to see."

"Can we go? Oh, please?" Pep begged, not all that convincingly.

"Maybe next time you go cross-country," said Dr. McDonald. "When I'm in the old folks' home."

"Then there's the U.S. National Tick Collection in Statesboro," Mrs. McDonald continued. "They have a machine that freeze-dries the ticks and coats

189

them with gold for better viewing under a high-powered microscope."

"Ticks are my favorite bug," Pep remarked. "They're *adorable*."

"Yeah, I'll bet you're a big fan of Lyme disease too," Coke told his sister.

"Cordele, Georgia, is the watermelon capital of the world," Mrs. McDonald said, closing her book, "and Claxton is the fruitcake capital of the world. But both of them are far to the south of where we're heading."

"Fruitcake needs a capital?" asked Coke.

Dr. McDonald pulled off the highway for a quick detour to the small town of Hartwell, Georgia, which was also named after Nancy Hart. But that's not why the McDonalds went there. The RV stopped alongside a historical marker and a stone monument. . . .

"The Cherokee Indians called this spot *Ah-Yeh-Li A-Lo-Hee*," said Mrs. McDonald, "or the center of the world. Many different trails radiated in all directions from this hub."

"Hub?" Coke said with a snort. "They should have called it the middle of nowhere."

"Where's the gift shop?" Pep asked. "This place is lame."

"That's the problem with kids these days," Dr. McDonald said. "You have no sense of history. When I was your age, we appreciated what happened before our time. I could name every state in the union, and all the state capitals too."

"Yeah, Dad," Coke said, "but there were only thirteen states back then."

Go to Google Maps (http://maps.google.com/).

Click Get Directions.

In the A box, type Hartwell GA.

In the B box, type 2319 Duncan Bridge Road, Sautee GA.

Click Get Directions.

Leaving Hartwell on the Lavonia Highway, road signs begin to appear for Gainesville, Georgia, which calls itself the chicken capital of the world.

"That's nothing to brag about," Coke said.

"Apparently they have a large number of poultry-processing plants there," Dr. McDonald noted.

"Please don't tell me you're going to take us to a poultry-processing plant," Pep said. "I will vomit."

"Hey, you should know what goes into the making of your food," Coke said.

"We're *not* going to take you to a poultry-processing plant," said Mrs. McDonald. "We're not even going to Gainesville."

"*Thank* you," said Pep.

"We're going to the Gourd Museum!"

"No!" both kids shouted.

"Wait, are you kidding me?" Coke asked. "Do you mean those gourd things that people put in baskets for no reason around Halloween time?"

"Yes!"

"They have a gourd museum?" asked Pep. "And *that's* the special place we're going to today?"

"No, the Gourd Museum is *on the way* to the special place we're going today," said Mrs. McDonald.

"It sounds fascinating," Coke said. "Can't we just drive off a cliff instead?"

The kids might not have been happy about it, but Dr. McDonald steered the RV along a series of small roads, passing through part of the Chattahoochee National Forest until he reached Duncan Bridge Road and the Gourd Museum.

"Can we wait in the car?" Pep asked. "This place

looks like it's going to be boring on steroids."

"Yeah, we don't care about gourds," said Coke.

"Suit yourselves," Mrs. McDonald said as she grabbed her camera. "Someday you'll regret that you came all the way to Sautee, Georgia, and you didn't go to the Gourd Museum."

"I guess I'll just have to live with the guilt," Coke said.

After her parents got out of the RV, Pep pulled out her notebook and got back to work on the cipher they had seen at the bottom of the swimming pool.

MOOVRETTHTOGO

She thought about it for a long time. Then she noticed the last four letters—TOGO. She remembered that the previous cipher they received had started with the same letters, but backward—OGOT. That couldn't be a coincidence. It had to mean something.

So she wrote out the entire cipher backward. . . .

OGOTHTTERVOOM

Then she started reversing each of the letter pairs, the strategy that had worked on the last cipher. . . .

GOTOTHETVROOM

"Go to the TV room!" she shouted.

"TV room?" asked Coke, who had been looking over her shoulder as she worked. "What TV room?"

"Do you think they have a TV room in the Gourd

Museum?" Pep asked.

They were about to hop out of the RV to find out when their parents came strolling back into the parking lot.

"Oh, you kids missed a good time," said their father as he opened the driver's-side door.

"I haven't had so much fun since the time we went to the Spam Museum," said their mother.

"Mom, do they have a TV room in the Gourd Museum?" asked Pep.

"A TV room?" Mrs. McDonald said. "Of course not. But they have two hundred gourds from twenty-three countries. It was fascinating. You should have seen the artwork created by the gourd artists."

"Gourd artists?" asked Coke.

As her father started up the RV, Pep turned to a blank page in her notebook and wrote the two ciphers they had received.

Go to Google Maps (http://maps.google.com/).

Click Get Directions.

In the A box, type 2319 Duncan Bridge Road, Sautee GA.

In the B box, type Atlanta GA.

Click Get Directions.

1. Go to the living room
2. Go to the TV room

It just didn't make any sense. Yet.

Leaving the Gourd Museum, the McDonalds got back on the road and drove right by Gainesville without stopping to look at any chickens. Dr. McDonald merged onto I-985 heading south, which soon merged with I-85.

Gradually the woods, lakes, trees, and mountain scenery of North Georgia started giving way to buildings, traffic, and road signs indicating the number of miles to Atlanta.

"I'm hungry," Coke said. "Can we stop for lunch soon?"

"Way ahead of ya," Mrs. McDonald said.

Before they reached the Atlanta city limits, she instructed Dr. McDonald to pull off onto a street called College Avenue. A few minutes later, they were rolling into the Waffle House parking lot.

"Waffle House?" shouted Coke. "I love Waffle House!"

"Oh, this isn't Waffle House," said his mother.

"It sure looks like a Waffle House, Mom."

"No, it's the Waffle House *Museum*!" she said triumphantly.

"No! Say it ain't so!" Coke protested.

"What's the big deal?" asked his mother. "We went to

the Gourd Museum. We went to the Spam Museum. We went to the Mustard Museum and the Pez Museum. What's the problem with a Waffle House Museum?"

"I'll tell you what the problem is," said Dr. McDonald. "We have too many museums. *Everything* isn't important. Everything doesn't deserve to have its own *shrine* dedicated to it. They probably have an air museum somewhere."

"Thank you, Dr. Grumpy," said Mrs. McDonald as they parked the RV outside the Waffle House Museum. "Why don't you lighten up a little and have some fun?"

Coke slung the backpack full of fireworks over his shoulder. Pep grabbed her Frisbee grenade.

"Do you really *need* that stuff?" Dr. McDonald asked Coke.

"I'm taking it, Dad."

Coke remembered that the last time he didn't take his weapons with him, a car nearly ran him over at Tunnelvision.

"Fine," Dr. McDonald said, throwing up his hands. He was still upset at the Dr. Grumpy remark.

The twins walked a few paces behind their parents.

"Keep an eye out," Pep whispered. "This is just the kind of place where Evil Elvis would show up."

"Trust me," Coke whispered back, "if he's behind the counter here, I'll blow this place to kingdom come."

As it turned out, Evil Elvis was *not* behind the counter. Instead, the McDonalds learned how the first Waffle House opened at this spot in 1955. Now there are more than fifteen hundred Waffle Houses all over the country, and each of them is open twenty-four hours a day, three hundred sixty-five days a year.

"They don't even need to put locks on the doors," Coke noted.

"Wow," Pep said as she read from a display case, "it says here that if you stacked up all the sausage patties that Waffle House serves in a day, it would be four times the size of the Empire State Building!"

The museum was actually quite interesting, but now the family was hungrier than ever. Fortunately, around the corner from the Waffle House Museum is . . . a Waffle House!

They walked over and were enjoying a perfectly normal, pleasant family meal, up until the moment that Coke received his second apple cinnamon waffle.

197

As he picked it up and was about to bite into it, he noticed that this was burned into the perimeter of the crust . . .

20-12-7-12-7-19-22-11-

12-12-15-9-12-12-14

"Oh no," he said. "Numbers."

The ciphers were coming fast and furious now.

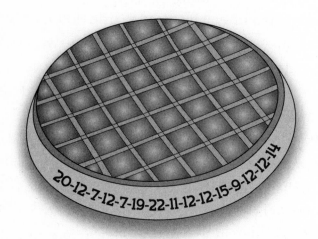

Chapter 24

THE SECRET FORMULA

"Oh, this one's a piece of cake," Pep said to her brother after they were back on the road. "I'll bet even *you* can solve it."

While their parents blasted an oldies station in the front seats, Coke examined the new cipher, which his sister had written down in her notebook.

20-12-7-12-7-19-22-11-
12-12-15-9-12-12-14

To Coke, it looked like a meaningless string of numbers. There were a bunch of twelves in there, and they repeated. But his brain was only good at storing and accumulating vast quantities of information.

It simply wasn't hard-wired to organize and process data. He handed the notebook back to his sister.

"Look, it's simple," she told him. "First you write out the alphabet. . . ."

A	B	C	D	E	F	G	H	I	J	K	L	M
N	O	P	Q	R	S	T	U	V	W	X	Y	Z

"Then you put a number below each letter. . . ."

A	B	C	D	E	F	G	H	I	J	K	L	M
1	2	3	4	5	6	7	8	9	10	11	12	13
N	O	P	Q	R	S	T	U	V	W	X	Y	Z
14	15	16	17	18	19	20	21	22	23	24	25	26

"The first number in the cipher is 20, so that must be a T," she said. "Then comes the number 12, and that's an L. After that is 7, which is the letter G. And then another L . . ."

"T-L-G-L?" Coke said. "That doesn't mean anything."

Pep did it again in her head, just to make sure she hadn't made a mistake. Coke was right. The message couldn't be TLGL.

She thought about it for a moment, and then brightened.

"Oh, I got it!" she said. "You need to put the numbers *backward*!"

Pep crossed out the first line of numbers and wrote it again, this time putting the number 1 below the letter Z and working back until the number 26 was below the A. Then she plugged in the corresponding letters to the numbers.

GOTOTHEPOOLROOM

"Go to the pool room!" Coke said, almost loud enough for his parents to hear. "What's *that* supposed to mean?"

"He wants us to go to a house or something," Pep replied. She added the new message to the list they had received so far.

1. Go to the living room
2. Go to the TV room
3. Go to the pool room

She looked to her brother, and all he could do was shrug his shoulders.

It was just eight miles on Dekalb Avenue from the Waffle House into Atlanta, the capital of Georgia. The McDonalds had not been to a big city since Washington, D.C. Coke and Pep craned their necks to look up at the tall buildings as they entered downtown Atlanta.

Dr. McDonald drove past Georgia State University and CNN headquarters on Marietta Street before

turning right toward Centennial Olympic Park, the site of the 1996 Summer Olympics. The Georgia Aquarium was on their left.

"Is *this* the special place you said you were taking us to today?" Pep asked. "Are we going to the aquarium?"

"No . . . ," Mrs. McDonald said as they drove along the north side of the park. "*This* is the special place we're going to today."

Across the street was a huge modern building, with the words WORLD OF COCA-COLA written on it.

"We took you to the Birthplace of Pepsi in North Carolina," said Dr. McDonald as he looked around for a parking lot. "So we figured it was only fair to take you to the birthplace of Coke too."

"This is *way* bigger than that lame Pepsi place," marveled Coke.

Pep wrinkled up her nose. She knew her brother was right, and she also remembered what had happened to her back at the Birthplace of Pepsi.

They parked the RV. Coke grabbed his backpack, and Pep grabbed her Frisbee grenade, just in case.

"Again with the backpack?" complained Dr. McDonald. "What do you keep in there, anyway?"

"My private stuff," Coke replied. "I like to have it with me in case somebody breaks into the RV."

"Nobody's going to break into the RV," his mother argued.

"I want it, okay?" Coke said.

Seeing as how they came to the World of Coke just for him, Coke's parents dropped the argument right there and started walking toward the building.

"Did you know that only two people in the world know the secret formula to Coke?" said Dr. McDonald.

"Really?" Pep said.

"Yeah. I read about it somewhere. In fact, those two guys aren't even allowed to fly in the same plane together."

"Why not?" Coke asked.

"Because if the plane crashed and they both died," Dr. McDonald told him, "there would be *nobody* who

203

knew the secret formula."

"I can't believe that," Coke said. "They must have written it down somewhere, or put it on a computer."

"That's the story I heard," said Dr. McDonald. "I don't know if it's true or not."

The World of Coke is a sort of combination museum and theme park. Dr. McDonald whined about having to pay money to see what was essentially a commercial for the Coca-Cola Company. He remarked that they should be paying *him*. But he went to buy tickets anyway. Next to the ticket office was a security station with serious-looking guards and a metal detector.

"They're looking through everybody's backpacks," Pep whispered to her brother. "You'll never make it through security carrying all those fireworks."

"I know," Coke said, and then called to his parents, "I changed my mind. I'm going to go put my backpack in the RV."

Dr. McDonald sighed and gave Coke the keys to the RV. Pep held on to her Frisbee grenade, knowing the guard would not be able to tell it wasn't an ordinary Frisbee.

"Why would you want to bring a Frisbee into the World of Coca-Cola?" her mother asked her.

"You never know when you might want to have a catch, Mom," Pep replied.

"Since when do you like Frisbee so much?"

"Like *forever*, Mom," Pep said, rolling her eyes. "What planet have *you* been living on?"

Dr. McDonald finished his transaction at the ticket booth, catching the end of the Frisbee discussion.

"Hey," he said, "how about we have a little catch right *now* in the parking lot while we're waiting for Coke to come back? Here, toss that thing to me, Pep. Lemme see if I remember how to throw it."

"No!" Pep said. There was no way she was going to let anybody touch her fifty-thousand-dollar Frisbee grenade. "Leave me alone."

Dr. McDonald could only shake his head. "Kids," he said.

After going through security, the first room the McDonalds entered told the history of Coca-Cola. Like Pepsi, Coke was invented by a pharmacist. His name was John Pemberton, and he was a Civil War veteran who lived in Atlanta. In May of 1886, he concocted the first batch of Coke syrup in a three-legged brass kettle in his backyard. He carried a jug of it down the street to Jacobs' Pharmacy, where it was mixed with carbonated water. They sold it for five cents a glass and claimed that it was not only refreshing but also

cured morphine addiction, headaches, and other ailments.

"Hey, Dad, maybe you should write a biography about the two guys who invented Coke and Pepsi," suggested Pep. "That would make a good book."

"Not a bad idea," said Dr. McDonald. "But it says here that John Pemberton never witnessed the success of Coca-Cola. He died just two years after he invented the stuff."

"That's sad," said Pep.

The World of Coke is huge, and the McDonalds wanted to see all of it. Milestones of Refreshment is a history of Coca-Cola memorabilia. In Search of the Secret Formula is a 3-D movie for kids in which your seat shakes and you get squirted with water. Bottle Works is a fully functioning bottling line. The Pop Culture art gallery features all kinds of artwork that uses the Coke logo. And of course, there's the Coca-Cola Store, where you can buy hundreds of products with the Coke logo.

For the twins, their favorite part was Taste It! on the upper level. You can sample sixty Coca-Cola drinks from all over the world, with names like Sparberry, Sunfill, and Inka. They even have a Coca-Cola Freestyle dispenser that lets you invent new drinks by mixing a hundred different flavor combinations any way you'd like.

While the twins were tasting all the drinks, their parents said they wanted to spend more time looking at the old Coca-Cola ads and artifacts through the decades. Everyone agreed to meet back at the RV in an hour.

Having ingested such a large quantity of carbonated beverages, Coke let out a burp that could be heard all the way across the Taste It! lounge. Pep was disgusted, but some of the other kids laughed.

"Hey, I have a great idea," Coke said.

"I don't like the sound of this already."

"Let's go find the secret formula for Coke!"

"You heard what Dad told us," said Pep. "Only two people in the world know the formula."

"Oh, give me a break," Coke said. "That's gotta be a myth. I'm sure it's written down somewhere in this building. Come on, let's go look for it."

"You're crazy!" his sister said as she followed her brother out of the room. "We'll get in trouble."

"You know," Coke said, "you'd get into a lot less trouble if you weren't always so worried about getting into trouble. Hey, look!"

There was a door near the corner with a sign that said AUTHORIZED PERSONNEL ONLY on it.

"I'm going in there," Coke said. "Come with me."

"I will not!" Pep said. "What would you do if you had the secret formula anyway? Mix up a batch down the basement and start your own soda company?"

"No," Coke told her, "I'd sell the formula to the highest bidder."

"Even if the secret formula *is* on a computer," Pep said, "I'm sure it's password protected. They have security here. They check the backpacks. You're not going to be able to just waltz right in there and find the secret formula so easily."

Coke started flapping his arms and making chicken noises.

"Buck buck buck buck . . ."

"Shut up!"

"Come on," Coke said. "I'll bet the secret formula is right beyond that door. Where's your sense of adventure?"

"I lost it at the Birthplace of Pepsi," she told him. "If you want to go looking for the secret formula so badly, go ahead. I'll meet you back at the RV."

With that, she walked away.

"You're no fun," Coke called after her. "Okay, fine. I'll go by myself."

Coke pulled opened the door marked AUTHORIZED PERSONNEL ONLY. It was pitch-dark inside.

"Grab him!" somebody yelled.

Chapter 25
THINGS GO BETTER WITH COKE

Four hands grabbed Coke. In seconds, his arms were tied tightly behind his back. He was pushed roughly into a chair and his legs were bound together. He struggled, but it was no use.

He felt his heart beating fast in his chest. How *stupid* it was to open that door, Coke told himself. He should have listened to his sister.

"It's about time we met," said the gruff voice in the dark. "My name . . . is Evil Elvis."

The light flicked on. There he was, just as Pep had described him—in a white jumpsuit, with a rubber

Elvis mask on his face. He took a long swig from a half-empty bottle of Coca-Cola.

"Help! Help!" Coke screamed.

"Save your breath," Evil Elvis told him. "Nobody can hear you."

The small room was empty, except for a wooden desk and a small trash can. Coke was being held from behind by the men who had tied him up.

"You!" Coke sputtered. "You scared my sister to death at the Birthplace of Pepsi!"

"Yes," said Evil Elvis, chuckling. "That was so much fun. And now it's your turn, Coke. Only this time, it will be more than just scaring. How fitting it is for me to kill you right here at the World of Coke. Everything that goes around comes around."

"What's *that* supposed to mean?" Coke just about spat out the words.

"Let him go, boys," said Evil Elvis.

Coke turned around to see two guys dressed in security officer uniforms. They looked like real security guys except for one thing—they were wearing bowler hats.

"The bowler dudes!" Coke hollered.

"At your service," snickered the one with a mustache.

"I thought you guys had changed," Coke said. "You

told me you had stopped harming kids and now you were into jousting."

The clean-shaven bowler dude snickered some more. "That's called lying," he said.

"So now you two work for Evil Elvis?"

"We work for whomever pays us," said the mustachioed bowler dude.

"Whoever," said Evil Elvis. "It's *whoever* pays us, you idiot!"

"Whatever."

"How did you know I was going to come in here?" Coke asked. "Was it the GPS chip?"

"That's how I knew you would come to *Atlanta*," said Evil Elvis. "Once you got here, I knew you wouldn't be able to resist opening a door that had a sign on it that specifically said not to open it. That's the way you are, Coke. You can't resist challenging authority. You thought you'd find the secret formula to Coca-Cola in here. I know all about you. I'm in your head."

Coke struggled against the ropes, but they were tight. He wished he had his backpack full of fireworks with him.

"Why don't you take off that stupid mask?" Coke said. "Show me your real face."

"You're not in a position to be telling anyone what to do," Evil Elvis correctly pointed out. He took a swig

from his bottle, then put it down on the desk. Then he pulled a little cigarette lighter out of his pocket and flicked it. He stared into the flame, mesmerized.

"Isn't fire beautiful?" Evil Elvis asked.

"It sure is, boss," both bowler dudes replied, snickering.

"I wasn't asking *you* morons!"

Coke recalled that his sister had mentioned something about Evil Elvis being a pyromaniac. But he thought it would be best not to encourage him in that direction.

"What's the deal with those ciphers you've been sending us?" Coke asked. "Go to the living room. Go to the pool room. What's that supposed to mean?"

"Oh, never mind my little messages," said Evil Elvis. "They would have been important if you hadn't come here. But I've got you now. So you can forget about all those rooms. You'll never need them. You're never going to leave *this* room. Well, at least not alive."

Evil Elvis tilted his head back and drained the last few ounces from the bottle. Then he held the lighter next to the edge of the bottle. The plastic started to smoke and melt. Coke looked up at the ceiling. There were no smoke detectors.

"Isn't it interesting how fire can destroy, and also create," Evil Elvis continued. "If I heat this bottle to a certain temperature with this flame, it will melt. Then I could mold it into just about anything. A child's toy, a tool, even another bottle."

Evil Elvis was obviously crazy. Coke looked around desperately for a way out. There were two doors—the one he had entered, and another one behind Evil Elvis.

"What are you going to do to me?" Coke asked, stalling for time.

"Oh, I have big plans for you, young man," Evil Elvis said as he flicked off the lighter and tossed the melted bottle into the garbage. "In fact, you're going to save the earth."

"Good one, boss!" snickered the bowler dudes, but Evil Elvis ignored them.

"Coke," he said, "do you realize that Americans go through two and a half million plastic bottles every *hour*? What a terrible waste. Fortunately a lot of those bottles get melted down and recycled. They're often made into roads, playground equipment, plastic lawn chairs and tables—"

"What does any of that have to do with *me*?" Coke shouted. "Why don't you leave me and my sister alone? What do you have against us? I never did *anything* to you!"

"Oh yes you did," Evil Elvis said, anger now in his

voice. "You most certainly did. Fellows, help our guest into the next room, won't you?"

"Sure thing, boss."

Evil Elvis opened the door behind him. The bowler dudes picked Coke up and carried him into the next room.

There were two large machines in there, connected by a conveyor belt of some sort. Coke guessed this was where the Coca-Cola was bottled, but he didn't see any bottles anywhere.

"How did you get into this place?" Coke demanded.

"Oh, let's just say I have connections."

The bowler dudes carried Coke over to one of the machines, which was about the size of a refrigerator. The other machine, to the left, was even larger. It had an opening at the top like a funnel, and the raised conveyor belt went around the perimeter of the room and fed into the opening.

"Do you know what a 3-D printer is, Coke?" asked Evil Elvis.

"A printer that prints in 3-D?"

"Oh, you're a smart one," Evil Elvis said sarcastically. "No wonder you were selected to be in The Genius Files program."

"Good one, boss!" said the bowler dudes.

"Using heat compression, a 3-D printer can take

empty soda bottles and spray the melted plastic through a tiny nozzle in successive layers to form a three-dimensional object," said Evil Elvis. "It uses a stepper motor and dual compact extruders."

"So what?" shouted Coke, struggling to get free. "What does that have to do with me?"

The bowler dudes snickered.

"Well, let me explain, Coke," Evil Elvis said calmly. "We all agree that recycling is a good thing, right? When we discard something we don't want or need anymore, the right thing to do is to recycle it, so it can be made into something else. Well, I don't want or need *you* anymore, Coke. So I'm going to recycle you."

"You're insane!"

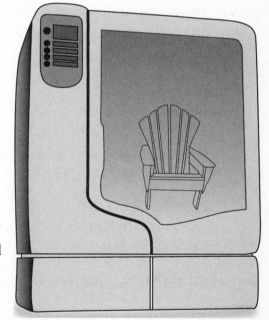

"What, would you rather I just bury you in a landfill?" asked Evil Elvis. "That wouldn't be very green of me, now would it?"

"You'll never get away with this!" Coke shouted. "Security will burst through those doors any second!"

The bowler dudes laughed.

"We *are* security," the clean-shaven one said.

"And we're already here," said the mustachioed one.

"Shut up, you idiots!" shouted Evil Elvis. "It was enough to say you *are* security! You didn't have to say you're already here! He *knows* you're here!"

"Sorry, boss."

Evil Elvis rubbed his forehead, then turned his attention back to Coke.

"I believe in freedom of choice," he said, almost in a kindly voice. "So I'll let you choose. Would you rather be recycled into a children's toy or a piece of playground equipment? Or maybe you'd like to be turned into a nice lawn chair for people to sit on? With a 3-D printer, you can be made into just about any object."

"You can't fool me!" Coke said defiantly. "That machine is a fake."

"Oh, it's the real thing, Coke."

"Good one, boss!" said the bowler dudes. "That was a Coke slogan, right?"

"Shut up!"

"If that thing uses melted plastic," Coke said, "you can't just put a *person* in and mold him into some other shape."

"Of course not," said Evil Elvis. "You can't take

plastic bottles and put them directly in the 3-D printer. First they have to be . . . shredded!"

See? I *told* you that eventually the story would involve Coke being thrown into a giant shredder! You didn't believe me!

Evil Elvis pointed to the even larger machine next to the 3-D printer. He flipped a switch on its side, and a whirring noise came out of it. It was vibrating. The raised conveyor belt began to move.

"There's a sensor at the top of the shredder that detects when something—or *someone*—has been inserted into the hopper," said Evil Elvis excitedly. "That turns on a series of high-torque, hydraulically powered rollers, which pull the object into the shredding chamber. This baby has a nine-hundred-horsepower Briggs & Stratton turbine engine in it, so once it grabs you, it doesn't let go."

"I don't want to hear it!" Coke shouted. "Why do you crazy people always feel the need to explain how you're going to kill somebody?"

"Well, that's all part of the fun, Coke."

"Good one, boss!"

"Shut up! Once inside the shredding chamber, Coke, your helpless body will encounter two sets of spinning, serrated blades made of high-grade chromium steel. They're set at an angle to cut one way

and then the other, so they'll chop your body into 6,093 tiny, unrecognizable particles. It's called cross-cutting. Isn't technology wonderful?"

"You're insane!"

"Coke, your mother drove all the way across the country to look at a frying pan. And *I'm* insane?"

"Good one, boss!"

"Leave my mother out of this!" Coke shouted.

"Enough talk," Evil Elvis said. "Hoist him up on the belt, boys!"

The bowler dudes each took one end of Coke's body and lifted him up on the conveyor belt, which went all the way around the room and ended directly in front of the shredder's gaping mouth.

"Stop!" Coke shouted as he moved along the conveyor belt. "Help!"

"Oh, I'm going to miss you, Coke!" said Evil Elvis. "It has been so much fun toying with you and your sister."

"You're a lunatic!" Coke screamed. His body was on the other side of the room now, turning the corner. "You're *worse* than Dr. Warsaw!"

"Thank you!" said Evil Elvis. "You couldn't have paid me a higher compliment."

"I'll do anything!" Coke begged. "Let me go!"

"The die is cast, so to speak," said Evil Elvis

excitedly. "The shredder will cut your body into pieces about the size of a kernel of corn. Those pieces will get mixed in with all the other plastic, which gets melted and fed into the 3-D printer. Then the printer will mold you into a lawn chair."

"I don't *want* to become a lawn chair!"

"What's the matter? Don't you care about the environment?" asked Evil Elvis. "Come on! Things go better with Coke."

"Good one, boss!"

Coke was three-quarters of the way around the room now. In about ten feet, he would drop into the shredder.

"Good-bye forever!" Evil Elvis said with a wave of his hand. "We must take our leave. I can't bear to hear the sound of a child being shredded. Let's go, boys."

The bowler dudes opened the door for Evil Elvis, and he skipped out jauntily, singing, *"I'd like to teach the world to sing, in per-fect har-mo-ny. . . ."*

"Help! Help!"

The conveyor belt advanced agonizingly slowly while Coke flailed around, trying desperately to free an arm or leg. When that didn't work, he tried to roll off the belt, even though success would mean falling

five feet to the ground, possibly onto his head. Even that would be preferable to falling into the mouth of the shredder.

The conveyor belt continued its relentless progress toward its final destination. Coke had expended just about all the energy he had, with no results. It looked like it was all over. His head was less than two feet from the shredder when the door suddenly flew open.

It was Pep.

"Coke!" she shouted. "What are you doing up there?"

"Never mind that!" Coke yelled. "Get me off!"

Pep grabbed the chair and pulled it over so she would have something to stand on. Then she grabbed Coke's shirt and tried to pull him off the conveyor belt.

"You're too heavy!" she shouted.

Coke's head was mere inches from the shredder when his sister gave one last desperate yank, ripping his shirt and sending him flying off the conveyor belt and landing on the hard linoleum floor with a thud.

"Ooooooooof!" he groaned when he hit the floor. "Will you be careful? I almost broke my leg."

"What happened?" Pep asked. "I was worried about you, so I came back."

"I'll tell you later," he said. "Get these ropes off me,

and let's blow this pop stand."

Pep untied the rope and they ran down the steps to the first floor, not slowing down until they were safely out in the parking lot.

"Where *were* you?" Dr. McDonald said when they got to the RV. "We've been looking all over!"

"I was learning about recycling," Coke said.

"What happened to your shirt, Coke?" asked his mother. "It's ripped to pieces! I wish you'd be more careful with your clothes."

"Well, I'm glad you're back," Dr. McDonald said as he reached into the cooler on the floor next to him. "Anybody want a Coke?"

"No!"

Go to Google Maps (http://maps.google.com/).

Click Get Directions.

In the A box, type Atlanta GA.

In the B box, type Summerville GA.

Click Get Directions.

Chapter 26

NATURE LOVERS

A s the RV pulled out of the parking lot, Coke and Pep sat in stunned silence.

"Wasn't that fun, kids?" Mrs. McDonald rhapsodized. "I had a fabulous time!"

"Yeah," Pep said glumly. "Fun."

The World of Coca-Cola hadn't been that much fun for Coke, especially when he was nearly shredded into tiny pieces and recycled into lawn furniture.

They got on I-75 heading north out of Atlanta and rode it for fifty-eight long miles, then took the exit for Route 140 West. As they were driving through

Chattahoochee National Forest—up in the northwest corner of Georgia—the GPS suddenly stopped working.

NO SIGNAL, it said.

Dr. McDonald had a pretty good sense of direction, and he enjoyed reading maps. But like most people, after he got a GPS he became dependent on it.

"How are we going to find the campground now?" he asked nobody in particular. "I don't know where I'm going. It's getting dark."

"Don't worry, Ben," said Mrs. McDonald. "We'll find the campground. I'll call them on the cell if we have to, and they'll direct us."

"This thing is a rip-off," Dr. McDonald said, giving the portable GPS a little slap with his hand. "It's supposed to cover the entire continental United States."

Coke and Pep, with problems of their own, hadn't been paying much attention. But when he heard the letters *GPS*, Coke looked up.

"Did you just say the GPS isn't working?" he asked.

"It's not getting a signal out here in the boonies," said his father. "It thinks we're in Siberia or someplace."

"Dad is worried that we're lost," said Mrs. McDonald.

"We're not lost!" shouted Dr. McDonald, who never considered himself lost. Being lost is a sign of weakness. Being lost isn't "manly."

Coke and Pep looked at each other. If the GPS in the car wasn't getting a signal, neither would the GPS chip that had been implanted in their scalps. That would mean Evil Elvis wouldn't be able to find them. So they were safe. For a while, anyway.

"This is beautiful country out here," Pep noted, gazing at the trees passing by. "Maybe we should stay here for a few days."

"Or the rest of our lives," added Coke.

They continued on, with Dr. McDonald getting progressively more apprehensive as each mile went by. Then, just when the forest came to an end, Mrs. McDonald noticed a little street sign on the left: SLOPPY FLOYD LAKE ROAD.

"Take a left here, Ben!" she said, just before they reached the intersection.

She knew she was right, because three miles down the road, nestled in a picturesque little valley near Summerville, Georgia, was the campground where she had made a reservation for the night—James H. "Sloppy" Floyd State Park.

"This is the place," Mrs. McDonald said as she hopped out of the RV.

"Sloppy Floyd State Park?" asked Pep. "What's up with *that*?"

"He was a Georgia politician," Coke inexplicably

remembered from an article he had read in *Newsweek*. "He served in the Georgia House of Representatives from to 1953 to 1974."

"You have no right to know that!" Pep shouted. "Nobody should know that kind of stuff!"

"I thought everybody knew that," Coke replied.

Dr. McDonald found the registration office and parked the RV. It was getting late and everyone was tired, so the McDonalds just had a quick snack instead of dinner and got ready for bed.

Knowing they were out of GPS range, Coke and Pep were able to sleep easy. There would be no middle-of-the-night visitors wearing Elvis masks or bowler hats. No secret messages to decode. No traps or large objects falling on top of them from high places.

"They can't find us here," Coke said to his sister just before dropping off to sleep.

In the morning, Mrs. McDonald made pancakes for everyone and they ate outside at a picnic table. Camping in a state park is a little different from the usual RV campground. More trees. More nature. Fewer people.

"Isn't it beautiful here?" Mrs. McDonald said, taking in a deep breath of clean air. "So quiet and peaceful."

"Do we have to leave right away?" asked Pep. "Can't we stay here awhile?"

"Yeah, we should move here permanently," said Coke.

"Actually, your mother and I thought it would be fun to do a little birding here before we got back on the road. The state park is known for birding."

"Hunting for birds?" said Coke. "Cool. Do we eat what we kill?"

"Birding is not hunting," said Mrs. McDonald sternly. "You *watch* the birds. Through binoculars."

I should mention here that Coke knew perfectly well that birding did not mean hunting and killing birds. Sometimes he just liked saying obnoxious things to annoy his parents. I'm sure you can relate.

"Watching birds?" he asked. "What's the point of *that*?"

"To appreciate the beauty of our winged friends," his father explained.

"I'd rather appreciate the *taste* of my winged friends," said Coke.

"Birding sounds boring," said Pep. "It sounds more boring than whale watching."

"Whale watching is *fun!*" said Mrs. McDonald.

"It would be more fun if you were allowed to shoot the whales," said Coke.

226

"Look, you two don't have to come birding with us," said Dr. McDonald as he took two pairs of binoculars out of the glove compartment. "You're big kids and you can be on your own for a while. But Mom and I are going."

The sky was looking threatening in the distance, but Coke and Pep weren't about to sit around the RV for hours waiting for their parents to come back. When they had checked in, the park ranger had given them a brochure that described several scenic hikes through the forest.

"Do you think we'll be safe if we go on a hike?" Pep asked.

"Nobody can bother us here," Coke said. "There's no GPS signal, remember?"

"Let's take our weapons, just in case," Pep said.

After grabbing the Frisbee grenade and Coke's backpack full of fireworks, they decided to hike the Marble Mine Trail, which leads to the entrance of an old mine where marble was quarried back in the days before the state park existed. They set out on the wide, well-marked trail into the woods.

After about a mile, Coke suddenly stopped in his tracks.

"Listen," he said. "Do you hear something?"

"No."

"Neither do I," he said. "It's perfectly quiet out here. I don't remember the last time I heard the sound of silence. Do you? Isn't that amazing? I can't wait to tell—"

"I could hear the silence if you'd stop talking," Pep said. And he did, for a minute.

"Think of it," Coke continued. "We're probably the only people for miles around."

"I wonder if there's a square inch in this forest where no human being in history has ever set foot," Pep said.

That's when she looked up and saw this carved into a tree . . .

OGAYOTAYETHAYUNGLEJAYOOMRAY

"You gotta be kidding me!" Coke shouted, looking around to see if the person who had carved the letters was still in the area.

"Calm down," Pep said. But her brother was furious now.

"Enough with the stupid ciphers!" Coke yelled into the woods. "Come and get us, Evil Elvis! What are you, chicken? Show your face, you coward!"

"Maybe that message is for somebody *else*," Pep said hopefully. "Maybe it's just some code the park rangers use. How could Evil Elvis know where we are, or that we would come to this exact spot?"

"Oh, he knew," Coke said, kicking the tree "Somehow, he knew. He knows *everything*. He knows what we're going to do even before we decide what we're going to do next. I hate him!"

Pep looked at the carving on the tree again.

OGAYOTAYETHAYUNGLEJAYOOMRAY

She didn't have her notebook with her to write down all the possible combinations. But after staring at the letters for a few minutes and seeing all those AY combinations, her face suddenly brightened.

"It's in pig latin, you big dope!" she said. "All you have to do is separate the letters into smaller words."

"Huh? I don't get it," Coke admitted.

"It's simple," Pep explained. "OGAY is GO in pig latin. OTAY means TO. ETHAY means THE. UNGLEJAY means . . . it's GO TO THE JUNGLE ROOM!"

"Cute," Coke said. "We're in the middle of a forest, and he says go to the jungle room. Another stupid nonexistent room we're supposed to find. This guy is driving me nuts. Let's get back to the RV before he jumps out from behind some tree."

"Wait a minute," Pep said, running to catch up with her brother. "Didn't you tell me that Evil Elvis said the ciphers didn't matter anymore?"

"That was because he had me tied up," Coke said. "He thought I would fall into the shredder and that

would be the end of me. But I got away. So the old ciphers matter, and now he's sending us *new* ones too."

When they got back to the RV, the first thing Pep did was open her notebook and add the new cipher to the list.

1. Go to the living room
2. Go to the TV room
3. Go to the pool room
4. Go to the jungle room

A few minutes later, it had started to drizzle outside and their parents came running back from their birding expedition.

"So how many birds did you kill?" asked Coke.

"Very funny," said Mrs. McDonald. "We spotted an eastern bluebird. It makes a sound like *true-ly true-ly*, in soft gurgling notes. Dad took some great photos."

"So," said Dr. McDonald, "should we get on the road, or do you kids still want to live here permanently?"

"No!" both kids shouted. "We hate nature. Let's blow this pop stand."

Go to Google Maps (http://maps.google .com/).

Click Get Directions.

In the A box, type Summerville GA.

In the B box, type Huntsville AL.

Click Get Directions.

Chapter 27

LET'S TURN IT UP A LITTLE

A thunderstorm was on the horizon as Dr. McDonald flipped on the wipers and steered the RV back on Route 48 heading west. To his relief, the GPS began working again as soon as he left the state park. It was a quick ten miles to the small town of Menlo, and from there just two miles until this appeared. . . .

"Woo-hoo!" yelled Coke. "Sweet home Alabama! Hey, can you

guys name two things that the following people have in common? Hank Aaron, George Washington Carver, Nat King Cole, Helen Keller, Joe Louis, Willie Mays, Jesse Owens, and Satchel Paige."

"They were all from Alabama?" guessed Pep.

"That's only *one* thing they have in common," Coke said. "The other thing was that they were all human beings."

"You're a moron."

"Don't call your brother a moron," said Mrs. McDonald.

She dropped her dog-eared copy of *Georgia Off the Beaten Path* into the garbage bag and took her brandnew *Alabama Family Adventure Guide* out of the glove compartment.

"What's the plan for Alabama, Mom?" Pep asked.

"It's starting to come down hard," said Dr. McDonald. "Let's keep the driving to a minimum today, okay?"

"Well, there's the MOOseum in Montgomery," said Mrs. McDonald. "It tells the history of beef and cattle. And they have a pest control museum in Decatur."

"Great," said Dr. McDonald with a groan. "A museum devoted to bugs."

"Let's see," Mrs. McDonald continued. "There's a spear-hunting museum in Summerdale. And at

the Hall of History Museum in Bessemer, they have Adolph Hitler's typewriter!"

"Why is Hitler's typewriter in Alabama?" asked Pep.

"It doesn't say," her mother replied. "Hmm, this is interesting. In the town of Sylacauga, there's a monument to a lady who got hit by a meteorite that crashed through the roof of her house in 1954. And in the same town, they have a tribute to Gomer Pyle. . . ."

"Who's Gomer Pyle?" the twins asked, in unison.

"Never mind," replied both parents.

"Well, you'll be pleased to hear that we're not going to *any* of those places," said Mrs. McDonald.

"Yay!"

"So where are we going?" asked Coke. "Wherever it is, it won't be much fun in the rain."

"Oh, you'll see," said his mother. "Stay on Route 117, Ben."

Outside, the sky was getting darker and more ominous. A few small towns passed by—Valley Head, Henagar—as they traveled across rural northern Alabama. It was pretty, but after a while pretty loses its appeal and the human brain yearns for "different" instead.

"Are we there yet?" asked Pep an hour after they had crossed the state line. "Color me officially bored."

They stopped for lunch at the side of the road near Guntersville Lake, but didn't get out of the RV because of the rain coming down. After lunch they switched to Route 72 West. It wasn't long before they reached the outskirts of a large city—Huntsville, Alabama. Dr. McDonald pulled off the highway just past the University of Alabama campus. A strange sight came into view: three or four huge, white rockets pointing toward the sky.

He pulled into a parking lot. The rain had tapered off a bit, but now there was lightning and the rumble of thunder in the distant sky.

"Is *this* where we're going today?" asked Coke.

"Yup," said Mrs. McDonald.

"Oh," Pep said, disappointed.

"Rockets are cool," said Coke.

"You think *anything* that ignites is cool."

"Well, anything that ignites *is* cool."

Huntsville, Alabama, is known as the rocket capital of the world.

It was here where the rockets were developed to put our astronauts in orbit around the earth and on the moon. Parts of the space shuttle and the International Space Station were designed here too.

"The U.S. Space & Rocket Center is a museum devoted to the space program," Mrs. McDonald read from her guidebook. "The Apollo 16 capsule is here, as well as a full-size replica of a Saturn V rocket. They have all kinds of interactive exhibits, demonstrations, and IMAX movies. They even have a rock that was brought back from the moon."

"Isn't this exciting?" Dr. McDonald asked, forgetting for a moment that teenagers don't get excited about anything their parents tell them is exciting.

It actually *was* exciting, but the twins weren't about to admit that.

Mrs. McDonald passed out ponchos for everyone to wear so they wouldn't get soaked in the rain. Coke was about to put on his backpack but stopped. If his fireworks got wet, they would be useless. Pep's Frisbee grenade would be ruined too. She had been specifically warned to keep it dry. Reluctantly the twins left their weapons in the RV and made a dash through the rain for the ticket window.

"Do you think they have any rides here?" Coke asked while they waited in line.

"No, they don't have rides here," Dr. McDonald replied, irritated. "It's not some silly amusement park. It's a *museum*. That's what's wrong with kids today. You can't enjoy anything unless you're staring at a screen or your body is being thrown back and forth in a little car. When I was a kid we used to go outside and—"

"Shush, Ben."

A flash of lightning lit up the sky.

At the ticket window, the lady behind the glass ran the credit card through her little machine and handed Dr. McDonald four tickets.

"I couldn't help but overhear your conversation," she said, "Actually, we *do* have two rides here at the U.S. Space & Rocket Center. I think you'll enjoy them."

"Yeah!" the twins yelled, with a fist bump. "Rides!"

"Can we go on the rides first?" asked Pep. "Please?"

"What are you kids, two years old?" Dr. McDonald said, thoroughly disgusted.

"Ben!"

"Okay, okay," he agreed. "You can go on the rides first. Go have fun. We'll catch up with you later."

"Yay!"

They made their way over to Space Shot, an amusement park-style ride in which a large group of people sit on chairs that wrap around a tall tower.

"This looks scary," Pep told Coke as they were strapped into their seats.

"Will you relax? It's just a *ride*."

A voice instructed the riders to "put your hands and feet out"—and at that moment the chairs were propelled 140 feet straight up in the air, in 2.5 seconds. Coke and Pep screamed, of course. It felt like they were in a rocket ship that had lifted off its launching pad. When they reached the top, they experienced pure weightlessness for a few seconds before Space Shot fell back to earth.

"That was *cool!*" Pep said when they were unstrapped from the seats. She was no longer fearful. "Let's go do the other ride!"

The G-Force Accelerator is in a round silver building that looks like a flying saucer. Before you go

inside, a sign near the entrance lists a bunch of medical issues that should prevent people from getting on the ride—motion sickness, asthma, heart problems, seizures, back

or neck pain, inner ear problems, detached retina, and so on.

"Do you think this thing is safe?" Pep asked.

"Of *course* it's safe!" said her brother. "They wouldn't have it here if it wasn't safe."

The twins were escorted into a large white tent.

"For your own safety," announced a disembodied voice, "inside the G-Force Accelerator, cross your hands over your chest. If at any point you feel sick, say the word *stop*, and the G-Force Accelerator will come to a stop."

"They just say that so you can't sue them afterward," Coke told Pep.

"If you don't have any questions," the voice continued, "you may proceed inside the G-Force Accelerator."

A door slid open with a *whoosh*, and the voice told them to enter the G-Force Accelerator. It was a round room that was larger and darker than the waiting room. There were about forty cushioned segments along the circular wall, half of them red and half of them blue. Coke and Pep were the only riders.

The voice instructed them to buckle themselves in tightly. There were no seats, just seat belts attached to the wall. It's a standing ride, in which you lean back slightly.

In the center of the room was a little booth where

a woman was sitting in front of a control panel. Her back was to the twins.

"Greetings!" she said into a microphone after the door had closed. "Welcome to G-Force Accelerator. This is the same type of simulator we use to help our astronauts train for a space flight."

"Does that voice sound familiar to you?" Coke asked his sister.

Before Pep could answer, the woman turned around in her chair.

"Mrs. Higgins!" Pep shouted. "No!"

Yes, it was *her*—the psycho who had set their school on fire, chased them through The House on the Rock, tricked them into causing a riot at Wrigley Field, and tried to blow their eardrums out at the Rock and Roll Hall of Fame.

"Well, look who's here!" said Mrs. Higgins, as cheery as can be. "My good friends the McDonald twins. What a coincidence! How nice to see you two again."

"Help!" Pep screamed, struggling to free herself from the seat belt. "Help!"

"Let us out of here!" demanded Coke.

"Oh, don't be such babies," Mrs. Higgins said as she pressed the spin button on the control panel in front of her. "This is going to be fun!"

The G-Force Accelerator started rotating slowly around Mrs. Higgins's booth in the middle.

"We walked right into her trap!" Pep said disgustedly. "I knew it! We *never* should have come here!"

Coke looked all around him for an opening. A door, a window, an emergency exit sign.

"See? It's not dangerous," Mrs. Higgins told them soothingly. "It's like one of those little teacup rides they have at kiddie amusement parks."

"I don't like it," Pep said. "And I don't like *you*."

"Let me tell you a little bit about G forces," said Mrs. Higgins as she turned a knob to make the room spin just a little bit faster. "You see, one G is the regular gravitational force we feel every day. Two G is twice that force, obviously. As the G force gets higher, it's almost as if you get heavier. So if you weigh a hundred pounds, at two Gs it feels like you weigh two hundred pounds. At three Gs it feels like you weigh three hundred pounds. And so on. See? This is not only fun, it's educational too."

The twins were beginning to feel a little dizzy as they spun around and around. Coke closed his eyes for a moment, but that made it worse.

"Why are you here?" demanded Pep as she felt her body press against the wall of the G-Force Accelerator. "You told us that you had stopped hurting children and you were into . . . uh . . . what was it called?"

"Spelunking," Coke said. "Exploring caves."

"Ah, you see one cave and you've seen 'em all," said Mrs. Higgins cheerfully. "That's the problem with spelunking. You could go away for a few million years, come back, and the cave would look exactly the same as it did the first time. Me, I like *action*. That's why I applied for the job here. Everything is in motion. Let's turn it up a little, shall we?"

"No!"

"Stop!"

She turned the dial in front of her, and the G-Force started spinning faster. The rumbling noise it made as it turned around got louder too.

"I'll bet you hardly even noticed when it went from two Gs to three right there," Mrs. Higgins said. "It's not so bad, is it?"

"Yes!" Coke yelled. He felt like a weight was bearing down on him and there was invisible pressure against his face. "It's bad! Turn it off!"

"The human body is an amazing machine, don't you think?" asked Mrs. Higgins. "Isn't it interesting to think about how much a body can endure? It all depends on the magnitude of the G force, the duration, the location, and the position of the body, you see."

"Shut up!" Pep screamed as she spun around and around. "We don't want to hear it!"

"One good slap to the face might have the force of a hundred Gs, but that doesn't kill anybody," continued Mrs. Higgins. "Yet the force of sixteen Gs for a minute can kill you, and so will seventy-five Gs for just one *second*. How are you two feeling over there?"

"I think I'm gonna puke!" Pep shouted. "I feel terrible!"

"Well, maybe now you know how *I* felt when you kids threw Dr. Warsaw out of The Infinity Room at The House on the Rock," said Mrs. Higgins. "Maybe now you know how *I* felt when he dumped me and got married to your aunt Judy instead."

"That wasn't our fault!" Coke screamed. "Leave us alone!"

"Oh no. Not now," said Mrs. Higgins. "This is too much fun."

"She's crazy!" Pep shrieked. "Do something, Coke!"

"What do you expect *me* to do?" he replied.

"Stop! Stop it!"

"Did you say go faster?" asked Mrs. Higgins. "Sure!"

She gave the dial another twist, and the G-Force Accelerator spun even faster.

"*Noooooooooooooooooo!*"

Coke tried to move his head left and right but

discovered he couldn't. The centrifugal force had pinned it to the wall. Similarly, his arms and legs were jammed in their positions. He was helpless.

"At four Gs, you start losing your color vision," Mrs. Higgins said gleefully. "Anything higher than that, and your lungs start to collapse, your esophagus stretches, and the blood starts to pool in your legs. Gee, I wonder how fast this thing can go?"

"That's enough!" Coke yelled. "We give up! We'll do anything you want! Just stop it! I want to get *off*!"

Pep shrieked again, but she was drowned out by the noise of the G-Force Accelerator.

"In space, no one can hear you scream, Pep," Mrs. Higgins said. "Eventually, you'll get to the point where you can't stand it anymore, and then we're talking about GILOC."

"What's GILOC?" Coke asked, fighting off the nausea that was beginning to overtake him.

"Gravity-induced loss of consciousness," explained Mrs. Higgins. "Your blood is pushed toward your feet. Your heart isn't strong enough to push it up to your brain anymore. The lack of blood flow gives you tunnel vision. And finally everything goes black. A-ha-ha-ha! I can't wait!"

The twins fought to conserve their energy and stay awake. The flesh on their cheeks was flapping like a

flag on a windy day.

"Are you still conscious?" Mrs. Higgins asked as they spun around and around her. "Wow. I'm impressed! You're pulling seven Gs now. At nine Gs, it will feel like your head weighs ninety pounds. And anything over ten Gs, well, your shoes come flying off your feet. Your teeth get pulled right out of your gums, one at a time. Your eyeballs go flying out of their sockets. Your arms get ripped off at the shoulders. Your internal organs—"

That's when the lights went out.

"Drat!" shouted Mrs. Higgins.

The G-Force Accelerator started slowing down. Gradually, the rumbling grew quieter. Finally the ride came to a complete stop.

"W-what happened?" Pep asked.

"I don't know."

Coke looked up. There was nobody sitting in the control booth.

"Where's Higgins?" he asked.

"She's gone," Pep replied.

The twins unstrapped themselves from their seat belts and stumbled out the door of the G-Force Accelerator like their bodies were made of rubber. Their parents were waiting for them at the exit.

"So was it fun?" asked Mrs. McDonald. "The electrical

storm knocked out all the power. The whole place shut down. It's a total blackout."

"I'll bet you kids are disappointed that the ride stopped in the middle, huh?" said Dr. McDonald.

"Yeah," Coke said, holding his head. "We should demand our money back."

Mrs. McDonald suggested getting some ice cream, but the restaurant—the Rocket City Grill—was closed because of the power failure. Even the gift shop had its doors locked.

After they had recovered their equilibrium, the twins managed to walk under their own power back to the parking lot. They were still nauseous, dizzy, confused, and more than anything else, exhausted.

"Where are we going now?" Coke asked, even though the only place he really wanted to go was to bed.

Dr. McDonald turned the key in the ignition.

"In the immortal words of Horace Greeley," he said, "go west, young man."

Go to Google Maps (http://maps.google.com/).

Click Get Directions.

In the A box, type Huntsville AL.

In the B box, type Tupelo MS.

Click Get Directions.

Chapter 28

FOLLOW YOUR NOSE

The rain was still coming down hard as Dr. McDonald pulled the RV onto I-565 out of Huntsville, Alabama, heading west. He could barely see through the windshield and almost missed the exit to turn onto Route 24. For the sake of safety, both parents agreed that it would be best to stop for the night as soon as possible. It took awhile to reach it, but they finally pulled into Slickrock, a campground in Russellville, Alabama. By dawn, the sky had cleared and they got back on the road early. Soon they were on I-22, when they saw this. . . .

"Woo-hoo," hollered Coke. "The Magnolia State!"

"Umm, can you smell the honeysuckle yet?" asked Mrs. McDonald.

"No, but I'm starting to smell the holding tank," her husband replied. "Coke, it's time you did a dump."

"Okay, okay, Dad."

"What are we going to do in Mississippi?" Pep asked.

"Can we go to Yazoo City?" asked Coke.

"What's in Yazoo City?" asked his father.

"I don't know," Coke said. "I just like saying Yazoo City."

Mrs. McDonald opened her *Road Guide to Mississippi* and started leafing through it.

"Let's see," she said. "Root beer was invented in Biloxi . . . Greenville is the towboat capital of the world . . . the International Checkers Hall of Fame is in Petal . . ."

"Oh, that sounds *real* interesting," Coke said, stifling a yawn.

" . . . the world's largest shrimp is on display in Pascagoula," Mrs. McDonald continued. "And oooh, look! The man who invented the dollar sign is buried near Pinckneyville!"

Dr. McDonald was getting increasingly irritated. With every offbeat destination his wife suggested, he would roll his eyes, shake his head, and let out a groan.

"The world's largest cedar bucket is in Oxford," Mrs. McDonald continued, "and in 1884, at a shoe store in Vicksburg, a man named Phil Gilbert came up with the idea of selling left and right shoes together in the same box!"

(Note to the reader: This stuff is *true*. I didn't make any of it up. Go ahead and Google it if you don't believe me.)

"How did they sell shoes before *that*?" Pep asked.

"One at a time, I guess," said Mrs. McDonald.

"Who would buy one shoe?" asked Coke. "A one-legged man?"

At that point, Dr. McDonald reached the point of exasperation. He grabbed the *Road Guide to Mississippi* out of his wife's hand.

"Tell you what," he said. "Forget about the stupid guidebook."

And with that, he threw *Road Guide to Mississippi* out the window.

"Ben!"

"Dad!"

"Our lives are too planned out," Dr. McDonald said. "That's what's wrong with the world today. We need a guidebook for *everything*. Why go anywhere anymore? You can just read about places in a guidebook or watch a video. Let's be spontaneous for a change. Let's just wing it!"

"I can't believe you did that, Ben!" shouted Mrs. McDonald. "I would *never* throw your things out the window."

"I can't take it anymore!" Dr. McDonald hollered, taking his hands off the steering wheel for a moment. "Who cares about root beer and checkers and how shoes used to be sold? I say we head west and follow our noses. That's what the pioneers did when they settled this country. They didn't have guidebooks.

They relied on their instincts."

In the back, Coke and Pep rushed to grab their cell phones so they could text each other.

Coke:

That was AWESOME!

Pep:

Dad is going mental

She may have been right. Dr. McDonald was not known for his spontaneity. He was a planner, a list maker, a scheduler, an alphabetizer.

But the family had been riding around in the little RV for more than two weeks now. If you take laboratory rats and confine them in an enclosed space for a long period of time, they start acting strange. They become aggressive; they fight and engage in other antisocial behaviors. People are no different.

For the next few minutes, the RV was filled with the unpleasant sound of angry silence. The twins were afraid to say anything. Mrs. McDonald was fuming. Her husband had never been a mean man, and it wasn't like him to act so impulsively. She felt lost without a guidebook, just like he felt lost without his GPS.

"I'm going to stop at the first decent-size town we come to," Dr. McDonald said, hoping to break the silence. "We'll get out and explore. You never know what you might find."

But there were no towns in sight—just a lot of nothing out the window on I-22. It wasn't until they had driven almost thirty miles that a sign finally came into view.

TUPELO

"Okay, we're going to Tupelo," Dr. McDonald announced, flipping on his turn signal.

"What's in Tupelo?" asked Pep.

"I have no idea," her father replied. "That's the beauty of it! We'll find out when we get there. Because that's the kind of adventurous, spontaneous family that we are. Right, gang?"

"Uh, yeah. Right, Dad," said Pep.

"Tupelo, here we come!" Coke yelled with fake enthusiasm.

"I have an idea," said Mrs. McDonald. "I'll Google Tupelo on my laptop. Then we can find out what sights—"

"No!" Dr. McDonald shouted. "No Googling! We're going to be spontaneous for once in our lives! I'm serious, Bridge. Open that laptop and I'll chuck it out the window."

"I think he means it, Mom," said Pep.

Mrs. McDonald resumed her fuming.

251

"I'll tell you something about Tupelo," Coke told the family. "Did you know that before the Civil War, Tupelo was called Gum Pond?"

"Thank you, Mr. Nobody Cares," said Pep.

Dr. McDonald pulled off the highway at exit 90 and began to meander around the small town of Tupelo. They passed a bedding store, a cemetery, a couple of restaurants, and a suburban neighborhood. After about five minutes of meandering, everybody had had enough of Tupelo.

"I hate to break it to you guys," Coke said, "but there's nothing going on here."

"Yeah, why did we come here?" asked Pep.

"Your *father* wanted to be spontaneous," said Mrs. McDonald, an edge to her voice.

"Spontaneity is boring," said Coke.

"See, Ben?" said Mrs. McDonald. "If you hadn't thrown my guidebook out the window, we could be going somewhere *interesting* right now. That's why I use guidebooks."

But a few seconds later, they passed a little sign.

ELVIS PRESLEY PARK

The twins looked at each other, panic in their eyes. Elvis Presley Park? If Evil Elvis was going to attack them anywhere, this would be the place.

"Hmmm," said Mrs. McDonald. "Why would they

name a park after Elvis Presley?"

"We don't want to go to that park," Coke shouted from the back. "It sounds boring."

But it was too late. Dr. McDonald had already made the right turn onto Elvis Presley Drive.

That's where they saw this. . . .

"I'll tell you why they named the park after Elvis Presley," said Dr. McDonald. "Because he was born here, in this very house!"

He pulled up to the curb near 306 Elvis Presley Drive and turned off the ignition.

"I don't think we should stop here, Dad," Coke said urgently. "It looks like a rough neighborhood. We

might get robbed."

"Yeah, it's probably boring too," said Pep. "Elvis was way before our time. I barely know who he was."

"Don't be silly," said Mrs. McDonald. "Elvis is universal, and timeless. Everybody loves him. This will be great for *Amazing but True*."

"See, Bridge?" said Dr. McDonald as he opened his door. "When you're spontaneous, you never know what you might run into."

"We're staying in here," Coke said as his parents got out of the RV.

"Yeah, we don't want to go in there," Pep agreed.

"Fine," said Mrs. McDonald brusquely as she grabbed her camera. She and Dr. McDonald walked up the sidewalk to the little white house, leaving the twins alone in the RV.

Too bad they missed the tour. Even though Elvis only lived in the tiny two-room house for a couple of years, it has been designated a Mississippi landmark. Dr. and Mrs. McDonald took the tour and also visited the grounds. There's a museum, a fountain, and a statue of thirteen-year-old Elvis holding a guitar. Surrounding the house is the Walk of Life—forty-two granite blocks representing each year of Elvis's life, with a little piece of information about what he did in that year. Also, nearby is the church where Elvis and his family worshiped. Inside, you can watch a video that shows what church services would have been like when Elvis was a young boy.

While their parents took their tour, Coke and Pep sat in the RV, worrying.

"I bet Evil Elvis is in there," Pep said, looking out the window. "I hope he doesn't hurt Mom or Dad."

"If we went in there, I'm sure he would try to kill us," said Coke.

Just then, there was a tap on the window at the other side of the RV.

"*Ahhhhhhhhhhhh!*" Pep screamed.

A policeman was looking at them through the glass.

"It's *him*!" Pep shouted. "Evil Elvis! He's dressed like a cop now! Get the fireworks ready, Coke!"

But it wasn't Evil Elvis dressed like a cop. It was a *cop* dressed like a cop.

"Do your parents know you're here by yourselves?" he asked after Coke rolled down the window.

"Yes, officer," Coke replied politely. "They'll be back any minute."

"This is a no-parking zone, y'know," the policeman said. "I'm gonna have to give your parents a ticket."

The officer wrote up the ticket on his pad and slipped it under the windshield wiper.

"It won't happen again, sir," Coke said.

"See that it doesn't."

The twins breathed a sigh of relief. They had gotten a ticket, but at least nobody had tried to kill them.

It wasn't until the policeman drove away that Pep got out of the RV and took a good look at the ticket. This is all it said . . .

$$\begin{matrix} N & T & A & O & T \\ E & I & T & T & N \\ D & O & I & H & I \\ R & N & D & E & O \\ A & G & E & M & G \end{matrix}$$

"It's not a ticket," Pep said. "It's a cipher!"

"You mean that cop wasn't a real cop?" asked her brother.

Pep didn't answer. She didn't care about who the cop was. She was already juggling the letters around in her head.

"It could be a twisted path cipher," she said after a few minutes of staring at it.

"What does that mean?"

"Look," Pep said, picking up a pencil, "don't think of the letters as going left to right or right to left. Think of them as being along a twisted path that can start at any letter."

She put the point of the pencil below the G on the bottom right corner of the cipher. Then she began to draw a line. . . .

"GO INTO THE MEDITATION GARDEN," Coke said as he followed the twisted path. "What's that supposed to mean?"

There was no time to discuss it because their parents came down the sidewalk and got in the RV.

"You kids should have come along," Mrs. McDonald said. "It was cool."

"Do they have a meditation garden in there?" Pep asked.

"No," replied her mother, "not that I know of."

Dr. McDonald put the key in the ignition and started up the RV. Then, quite suddenly, he looked up for a moment and turned off the motor. He sat there motionless, staring out the windshield at the Elvis Presley birthplace with a faraway look in his eyes. It seemed like he was in a trance.

"Ben, are you okay?" asked Mrs. McDonald.

"What's the matter, Dad?" asked Pep, alarmed.

"I think he might be having a stroke!" said her mother. "Call 911! I'll go get help!"

But before she could even pull the door handle, Dr. McDonald snapped out of it.

"I've *got* it!" he said excitedly.

"Got *what*?" they all asked.

"I just figured out what I should write my next book about."

"What, Dad?"

"I'm going to write a biography of Elvis Presley."

Coke and Pep looked at each other, horrified looks on their faces.

"That's a *wonderful* idea, Ben!" said Mrs. McDonald. "Elvis started out dirt poor in this little house and became one of the most famous people of the twentieth century. He died tragically. You can use your history background. You love his music. . . ."

"It will sell like crazy!" Dr. McDonald said. "A lot better than *The Impact of Coal on the Industrial Revolution*."

As their parents got more and more excited with the idea, Coke and Pep got more and more upset. That's all they needed—their dad researching the life of Elvis while Evil Elvis was trying to kill them.

"I think it's a terrible idea, Dad," Coke said. "Nobody cares about Elvis anymore. He died like forty years ago."

"Yeah," Pep agreed, "and besides, there are probably *hundreds* of books about Elvis Presley."

"That just proves people have a hunger to read about him," Dr. McDonald said. "But mine will be better. I'll find out everything there is to know about him. I'll write the *definitive* biography of Elvis. Mark my words, this will get me on the bestseller list."

He had a dreamy look on his face as he started up the engine again and pulled away from 306 Elvis Presley Drive.

If you wanted to find out everything there is to know about Elvis Presley, there's one place you'd need to go.

Graceland. Elvis Presley's house. Memphis, Tennessee.

Go to Google Maps (http://maps.google.com/).

Click Get Directions.

In the A box, type Tupelo MS.

In the B box, type Memphis TN.

Click Get Directions.

Chapter 29

GRACELAND

Mrs. McDonald pulled the road atlas out of the glove compartment and spread it across the dashboard. She was thrilled to see that Tupelo, Mississippi, was only about a hundred miles from Memphis. Unless they hit some unexpected traffic along the way, they would be in Tennessee in less than two hours. Graceland was just a few miles past the state line.

She got on her cell phone and found out that there was an RV campground right across the street from Graceland. Perfect!

While he drove, Dr. McDonald's face showed a sense of calm and glassy-eyed peacefulness that hadn't been there for a long time. He was humming the old Paul Simon song. . .

"Graceland, Graceland, in Memphis, Tennessee. I'm going to Graceland. . . ."

In his head, he had already started planning out his Elvis biography. The first chapter would begin on the day Elvis and his twin brother, Jesse, were born in Tupelo. The chapter would end that very same day, when Jesse died during childbirth.

In the back of the RV, meanwhile, the twins realized there was nothing they could do to avoid a trip to Graceland and an inevitable confrontation with Evil Elvis. They were nervously preparing to go to war.

Coke carefully read the instructions on his fireworks so he would know how to light them, aim them, and shoot them. Pep was loosening up her throwing arm. She knew it might be up to her to take out Evil Elvis with the Frisbee grenade. She would only get one shot, so it would have to count. She felt like Luke Skywalker preparing for the dive into the Death Star.

The twins had a few other "weapons" at their disposal, but it wasn't like they would be much help in a fight: One roll of duct tape. A can of Silly String.

Two yo-yos. A jar of bubbles. A can of Spam they got at the Spam Museum in Minnesota. A can of alliga-

tor repellent. If worse came to worst, they could hit somebody with the POUPON U toilet seat their mother had bought them back at the Mustard Museum in Middleton, Wisconsin. It was pretty hard.

They were speeding along I-22, traveling west and north diagonally across the state of Mississippi. Dr. McDonald didn't look like he was going to stop for food, drink, or to stretch his legs. He was a man on a mission. The countryside was flying by at sixty miles per hour, and nobody was paying much attention to the scenery.

Shortly after they drove through Holly Springs National Forest, they passed this. . . .

When they crossed the state line and there was no exuberant outburst from the backseat, Mrs. McDonald turned around to see if anything was wrong.

"No woo-hoo?" she asked. "No facts about Tennessee? It's the Volunteer State, you know."

"I volunteer to go home," Coke said glumly.

Minutes later, they reached the outskirts of Memphis. Dr. McDonald noticed the gas tank was close to empty, so he pulled into a station to fill it. When he started up the engine again, the GPS indicated they were just a few miles from Graceland. He made a left onto East Shelby Drive and drove a short time before he came to a street marked ELVIS PRESLEY BLVD.

"This is it, Ben," Mrs. McDonald said. "Make a right here."

It wasn't a fancy neighborhood, as they had expected. There were no other mansions around, and few houses at all. Most of the buildings on the street were pawn shops, gas stations, fast-food restaurants, and motels. They knew they were getting close to Graceland when they passed the Elvis Presley Boulevard Shopping Center and a Days Inn motel with a sign out front that said . . .

"Before Elvis there was nothing."

—JOHN LENNON

"I'm so excited!" said Mrs. McDonald.

Just past that motel, they saw this on the left. . . .

"This is it!" said Dr. McDonald, and he began singing "Hound Dog." The kids groaned.

Directly across the street from Graceland is a hotel called—naturally enough—the Heartbreak Hotel. And directly behind the hotel is a large campground filled with RVs. Dr. McDonald pulled into the parking lot. Mrs. McDonald got out and went to check in at the office.

"I think we're gonna need this," Coke whispered to his sister as he grabbed his backpack. But his father stopped him.

"Do you really think they're going to let you take that backpack into Graceland?" he said. "It's like a museum. Use your head, Son."

Coke looked to Pep.

"I'll take my Frisbee," she said.

"You take that thing *everywhere*," said Dr. McDonald, "and I haven't seen you throw it once."

"I have a feeling I'm going to throw it this time, Dad."

Coke stashed his backpack in the RV and shut the door. It was going to be up to Pep to defend them this time.

Mrs. McDonald returned from checking in at the office. The whole family walked through the parking lot of the Heartbreak Hotel and followed signs to the Graceland ticket window.

There were a few tour options. In addition to seeing Elvis's home, visitors can also visit the Elvis Presley Car Museum, which includes thirty-three cars, motorcycles, go-carts, dune buggies, and other vehicles owned by Elvis. There's also an optional tour of his private jet, the *Lisa Marie*, which has a living room, a bedroom, gold-plated seat belts, suede chairs, leather-covered tables, and twenty-four-karat gold-flecked sinks.

"Doesn't that sound cool?" asked Mrs. McDonald.

"No," the twins replied in unison.

"You kids are so grumpy," she told them. "I wish you'd try to get into this. You're going to remember this experience for the rest of your lives."

"I'll bet we will," Coke replied.

Dr. McDonald bought the tickets and handed one to each of the twins.

"Okay, I think you kids should take the Graceland tour first," he told them. "Mom and I need to speak with somebody in the office about researching my book."

Coke and Pep looked at their parents with sad puppy-dog eyes.

"We'll meet up later," Mrs. McDonald said. "You kids wouldn't want to hang around with old fogies like us anyway."

"We want to go with you old fogies," Pep whined.

"You know what?" Dr. McDonald said. "This is ridiculous. You kids are thirteen years old now. It's time for you to show a little independence. You don't need us leading you around like you're toddlers. How are you going to make your way in the world if you follow us everywhere? That's what's wrong with kids today."

"But we're scared," Pep admitted.

"Scared?" said Mrs. McDonald. "That's crazy. This place is like Disney World."

Yeah, if Mickey Mouse was a mass murderer.

Their parents said good-bye, and Coke and Pep walked away, dragging their heels. They stalled for a few minutes to look in a gift shop that sold Elvis

playing cards, spoons, T-shirts, mints, photos, videos, CDs, dolls, nail files, back scratchers, and just about every product imaginable with a picture of Elvis Presley on it.

"Elvis is probably making more money dead than he ever did alive," Coke commented.

Finally the twins got on the shuttle bus that would take them across the street to Graceland. Nobody else was on the bus.

"Maybe everything will be all right," Pep said hopefully. "Maybe Evil Elvis isn't even here, and we got all worked up over nothing."

"Where is everybody?" Coke asked the bus driver.

"Oh, it's pretty quiet today," she replied. "Most of the tourists are from the Professional Elvis Impersonators Association."

"The *what*?!" Pep asked.

"The Professional Elvis Impersonators Association," said the bus driver. "They're a real group, and about a hundred of 'em are here already, with more on the way. They come in costume and everything. I'll tell ya, those guys are nuts."

"We know," said Coke.

It was a quick trip across the street. The bus drove up the winding driveway that cut across the front lawn and stopped in front of Graceland.

The colonial-style house, with four white columns, wasn't quite as grand as the twins expected. It looked a little like a town library. But the lawn and landscaping were perfectly manicured. A plaque out front said the house had been built in 1939 and it was on the National Register of Historic Places.

There was a uniformed guard standing around to help people with questions and directions.

"So this is it, huh?" Coke asked as he got off the bus.

"Yup," the guard said. "Elvis bought this house when he was just twenty-two years old, and he paid a hundred thousand dollars for it."

You, dear reader, probably don't know or care how

much a house costs today. There's no reason why you should. But a place like Graceland—even without a famous owner—will go for many *millions* of dollars.

"Where do we go first?" Pep asked the guard.

"Go to the living room."

"Wait. What did you say?"

"Go to the living room," said the guard, pointing to the right of the front steps.

Coke turned to Pep.

"That was the first cipher!" they said simultaneously.

There were two white statues of lions on the side of the front steps. The twins climbed the steps slowly, looking all around for trouble.

"Okay," Coke said, "let's find Evil Elvis, take him out with the Frisbee before he can lay a hand on us, and blow this pop stand."

"Sounds like a plan," Pep agreed.

Coke pulled open the door and saw four Elvis impersonators—with white jumpsuits and slicked-back hair—in the front hallway. He tensed up instinctively.

"Throw it, Pep!" Coke said, "Let's kill them all!"

"Calm down!" Pep said, holding her brother back. "None of them are Evil Elvis."

"How do you know?"

"They're not wearing masks," she explained.

The Elvis impersonators were weeping at the

sight of Elvis's living room and consoling each other. Coke and Pep entered the house cautiously. She held her Frisbee grenade tightly, ready to let it fly at any moment.

The living room was almost all white—white rug, white chairs, and a long white couch. There was a big mirror over the fireplace, and two big stained-glass peacocks on the doors. A rope across the doorway prevented visitors from going into the room.

"This is where his funeral service was held," said one of the weeping Elvises, and that made them sob all the more.

Outside the living room, there were steps leading upstairs, but the second floor was closed to the public. Just past the living room was a smaller music room with a black grand piano. Three more Elvis impersonators were in there, speaking in solemn tones and dabbing their eyes with tissues.

The twins walked cautiously down the hall on the right to Elvis's parents' bedroom and then across the foyer to the dining room and the kitchen. There were several more Elvis impersonators there.

"This place is *crawling* with Elvises!" Coke told Pep. "How will we know when we see Evil Elvis?"

"We'll know."

It wasn't clear which way to go next, so Pep asked

one of the guards.

"Go to the TV room," he said, pointing downstairs.

Coke looked at his sister.

"That was the second cipher!"

They walked down the steps. To the left was a room with three old-time TV sets side by side, presumably so Elvis could watch three channels at the same time. There was yellow carpet on the floor, a lightning bolt painted on the wall, and a sculpture of a white monkey on the coffee table. It was getting creepy, and Pep grabbed Coke by the elbow.

To the right of the TV room was a small room with folded multicolor fabric on the walls and ceiling. In the middle of the floor was a pool table.

"The third cipher said to go to the pool room!" Coke recalled. "That means the jungle room will be next."

And so it was. They climbed the steps again to the most unusual—some would say *weirdest*—room of them all. There was green shag carpeting, not just on the floor but also on the *ceiling*. A waterfall filled one wall, and oddly carved wooden chairs covered with animal fur were scattered around the room.

From there, a door led outside. There had been no sign of Evil Elvis inside Graceland.

"He's not here," Pep said hopefully as they walked into the backyard.

"Don't let down your guard," Coke warned his sister. "Be ready with the Frisbee."

Graceland has a huge backyard with horses grazing behind a white fence. More Elvis impersonators were wandering around the grounds. The twins looked them over carefully and decided they were not a threat.

The path led to two separate buildings out back. The Hall of Gold was filled with gold records on the walls, stage costumes, and posters from Elvis movies. The racquetball building once had a full-size court, but now houses more awards, memorabilia, and photos.

That was it. They had toured every room and every building at Graceland. There had been lots of Elvis sightings, but no sightings of Evil Elvis. Even so, the twins refused to relax. There was the sense of a lurking presence everywhere, a sense of impending doom that never went away.

"I have a bad feeling," Pep said.

"So do I," said her brother.

That's when they saw this. . . .

"That was the last cipher," Pep said. "Go into the meditation garden."

The path led around to the south end of the house, where there was a kidney-shaped swimming pool. It was smaller than you would expect for such a famous celebrity. Behind the pool was a circular fountain and a statue of Jesus.

"This is it," Coke said solemnly as they entered the meditation garden. They were alone.

There were four graves in front of them, laid out side by side in an arc—Elvis, his mother, his father, and his grandmother. There was also a little memorial to his twin brother, Jesse. Flowers had been placed all around, along with notes sent by fans. At the top end of Elvis's tomb was an eternal flame that danced in the wind.

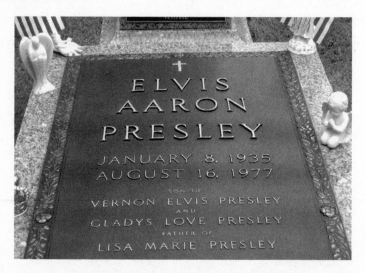

"He's down there," Pep said quietly as they stood in front of the tomb. "Six feet under."

A few Elvis impersonators strolled into the meditation garden and immediately began sobbing at the sight of Elvis's grave.

"Maybe we should say a prayer or something," Coke whispered to his sister.

They closed their eyes and prayed silently. When they opened them again, a figure was standing at the other side of Elvis's tomb, behind the flickering flame, his arms crossed in front of him.

It was Evil Elvis.

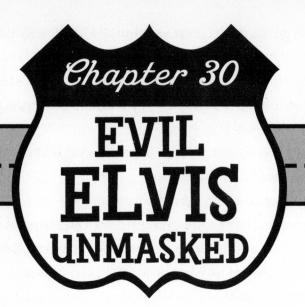

Chapter 30

EVIL ELVIS UNMASKED

"**I** love an eternal flame," Evil Elvis said. "Don't you?"

"Ahhhhhhhhh!" Pep fell back as if she had been hit by a strong gust of wind.

There was nowhere to run. There were two Elvises on either side of them, and they weren't crying any-more. They had their arms crossed, and they were glowering.

"Be ready to throw the Frisbee grenade," Coke whispered to Pep. "This is our chance to get rid of him once and for all."

"I've got to hand it to you kids," Evil Elvis said. "I never thought you would make it out of the World of Coke alive. And after you did, I was *sure* the G-Force Accelerator would be the end of you. But here you are. You know what? You've got spunk."

Coke was about to say something, but Evil Elvis wasn't done.

"I *hate* spunk," he added.

Pep fingered the Frisbee grenade, pushing on the power button. She was waiting for the perfect moment to fling it and hoping that her aim would be true.

"Why do you hate us so much?" Coke asked. "We never did anything to you."

But Evil Elvis wasn't in the mood to answer questions. He had his own agenda.

"It's such a shame that Elvis Presley had to die so young," he said. "The same will be said about you two."

Coke looked left and right, searching for an escape path in case Pep missed with the Frisbee grenade, or if it failed to detonate. Pep tightened her grip on the Frisbee.

"Who are you, really?" Coke asked. "Why don't you take off that silly mask and show your face?"

"We all wear a mask, don't we?" said Evil Elvis. "You pretend to be a couple of sweet, innocent kids on

vacation with your parents. But you're cold-blooded killers. That's what you are. You killed Archie Clone in Washington, and you nearly killed Dr. Warsaw in Wisconsin."

That voice! Coke had heard it before and tried to place it. It sounded strange, like Evil Elvis was trying to disguise his real voice.

"What are you going to do to us *here*?" Coke asked. "Stomp us to death with your blue suede shoes?"

Evil Elvis laughed.

"No, you would only find some way to escape," he replied. "I'm tired of playing games with you. I have a simpler idea. Do you know what Elvis used to do when he didn't like what was on TV?"

"Change the channel?" Coke guessed.

"No," said Evil Elvis. "He would shoot the screen."

With that, he reached into his pocket and pulled out a pistol.

"*Now*, Pep!" Coke shouted.

Pep quickly jumped into position, brought back her arm, and whipped the Frisbee *hard* at Evil Elvis. The Frisbee hit him on the wrist and ricocheted off, landing in the swimming pool behind him. The gun fell out of his hand and went off when it hit the ground.

"You little punks!" shouted Evil Elvis.

"Run!" Coke shouted.

"Get them!"

There was a driveway next to the meditation garden that went alongside Graceland and out to the street. Coke and Pep took off in that direction, pursued by Evil Elvis and four other Elvis impersonators.

"Where are we going?" Pep yelled.

"I don't know!" Coke yelled back. "Follow me!"

When they made it around to the front of the mansion, they had about five steps on the closest Elvis impersonator. A shuttle bus was waiting to take visitors back across the street. But the twins didn't get on it. With Coke running in front, they dashed across the huge lawn, out the gate, and into Elvis Presley Boulevard.

It's a wide street with four lanes of traffic, and cars were whizzing by in both directions. Grabbing his sister's hand, Coke ran out into the street anyway. A blue Toyota swerved out of the way at the last instant and avoided hitting them by inches. There was honking and cursing from the drivers.

"Watch out!"

"What are you kids, nuts?"

Coke and Pep dodged three more cars, almost

getting run over several times. One of the cars screeched to a halt and got rear-ended by the truck right behind it. That provided a screen to slow down the Elvises, who were already huffing and puffing. Coke and Pep made it to the other side of the street unscathed.

"Come on!" Coke said to his sister. "We can hide in the RV!"

Pep turned around for a moment to look behind. The Elvises were still trying to cross the street.

The twins ran past several souvenir stores, around the back of the Heartbreak Hotel, and into the campground behind it. It took them a minute or two to find their RV among the dozens of them parked out there, many of them looking identical.

Coke yanked open the side door, thankful that their parents usually forgot to lock it, and climbed inside. Pep slammed the door behind them.

They got down on the floor so they couldn't be seen through any windows. They were breathing heavily and sweating, their hearts pounding.

"You were supposed to—"

"*Shhhhhhhh!*" Pep warned her brother. "He might hear us!"

"You were supposed to skip the Frisbee grenade off the *ground*!" Coke whispered. "Don't you remember?

It was programmed to explode on the *second* impact."

"I forgot," Pep whispered. "I panicked. You should be thankful that I knocked the gun out of his hand."

"Okay, we're safe here," Coke whispered.

"What do we do *now*?"

"Nothing," Coke said. "We wait for Mom and Dad to get back. Then we'll get out of here."

Cowering there on the floor of the RV, it felt like an hour had passed. In fact, it was only a few minutes. They listened carefully for noises outside but only heard the sound of a jet overhead.

Coke reached over for his backpack full of fireworks. The more he thought about it, the more he realized that buying all that stuff had been a big mistake. He should have known that he wouldn't be able to bring the backpack into any museums or public buildings that had security. Even if he could, it would have been impossible to open the backpack the instant they were threatened, take out the fireworks, light them, and get away without blowing himself up. That was a hundred dollars' worth of fireworks wasted.

Five minutes had passed since they had been hiding in the RV.

"I think we lost them," Pep said.

That's when the door opened.

It was Evil Elvis.

"Ahhhhhhhhhhhhhh!" Pep screamed. "Coke! Do something!"

"Well, *here* you are!" said Evil Elvis. "I've been looking all over for you two."

Coke decided the only defense was a good offense. He jumped on Evil Elvis, flailing wildly at him with both fists.

"Leave us *alone!*" Coke shouted.

While Coke and Evil Elvis wrestled on the floor, Pep managed to find the can of Silly String, and she started spraying it all over Evil Elvis's mask. When that didn't seem to work, she got out the can of alligator repellent she had bought at South of the Border and started shooting it at Evil Elvis. He grabbed the can and flung it toward the driver's seat.

"No more Mr. Nice Guy!" he said, fending off Coke's blows. "You two are *dead!*"

Pep tried to open up the bubble jar that Bones and Mya had given them so she could throw the bubble soap into Evil Elvis's eyes and blind him, but she couldn't twist the top off. She tried to hit him over the head with a can of Spam, but it went flying out of her hand. She looked around desperately for something she could use as a weapon.

The POUPON U toilet seat that her mother had gotten

at the Mustard Museum!

Pep grabbed it and swung it at him, but she got off-balance and only delivered a glancing blow.

"That's *enough*!" Evil Elvis shouted, ripping the toilet seat out of Pep's hand and brandishing it like a baseball bat.

Coke fell back, exhausted. His shirt was ripped. He had no fight left in him.

Evil Elvis reached into a pocket, the same pocket he had pulled a gun from in the meditation garden.

This was it. The twins were done for. It was over. Now Coke was *really* mad.

"I can't believe you forgot to lock the door!" he yelled at his sister. "This is all *your* fault!"

"I thought *you* locked it!" Pep shouted back.

"How could I lock it?" Coke yelled. "You came in after me!"

"There's no reason to bicker, kids," Evil Elvis said. "It doesn't matter who was supposed to lock it. You'll both be dead soon."

Instead of pulling a gun from his pocket, he pulled out a cigarette lighter and flicked it on.

"Before I seal up the door from the outside and drop this in the gas tank," Evil Elvis said, "it's only fair to let you know who was responsible for killing you."

With his other hand, he peeled off the Elvis mask

and fake Elvis hair. It turned out that *he* was a *she*.

"AUNT JUDY!" shouted the twins.

"That's right, you little twerps!" Aunt Judy said, now using her normal female voice. "And I thought you two were so smart."

"But you're our aunt!" shouted Pep. "Why would you want to hurt us? Our mother is your sister!"

"And you know what?" Aunt Judy said, "I always hated my sister. I couldn't believe she actually had the nerve to show up for my wedding. There's only one person I care about—Dr. Herman Warsaw. My husband. Oh, I wish I could see the look on my sister's face when she finds your bodies in here."

Coke clutched his backpack to his chest. Slowly he moved his hand until he found the zipper. The fireworks would be their only chance.

"Dr. Warsaw told you to kill us?" Pep asked, trembling.

"Let's just say Hermy suggested that while he's recuperating from his injuries—injuries that *you* caused, by the way—I could, shall we say, take matters into my own hands."

"But I thought you were on your honeymoon!" Pep said.

"Oh, we will be," Aunt Judy said. "Just as soon as you two are dead. Then our minds will be at ease and

A few seconds later, that's exactly what happened. One of the rockets damaged the floor of the RV and made a tiny puncture in a seam of the gas tank, which had been filled to the brim a few hours earlier. When a burning cinder fell through the hole, the tank exploded in a huge orange fireball, with wood, metal, and burning debris flying in every direction.

By the time the fire department arrived, there wasn't much left except for some twisted metal and tires, which were still burning and giving off an awful-smelling stench. Everything else was burned beyond recognition.

Coke and Pep didn't stop running until they got to the entrance of the campground. Exhausted and still in a state of shock, they sat on the bench there, catching their breath while the RV burned. Lots of people had gathered around to see the fire, but nobody paid any attention to the twins.

"Well," Coke finally said, "I guess we don't have to worry about Evil Elvis anymore."

A few minutes later, their parents came strolling back from their tour of Graceland.

"Great news!" Dr. McDonald told the kids. "I spoke with some people in the office, and they're going to

let me look at Elvis's personal papers for my book. Hey, what happened to you two? You're a mess."

"It's a long story," Coke said.

"I can't believe you ripped *another* shirt!" said Mrs. McDonald. "Why can't you take better care of your clothing? I wish you would be more careful."

"Come on," Dr. McDonald said, throwing an arm around each of the twins, "let's go back to the RV."

"Umm, yeah, about the RV . . ."

EPILOGUE

What?! Are you kidding me? They blew up the RV? And Evil Elvis was Aunt Judy the whole time? I didn't see *that* coming!

What happened to Mrs. Higgins? Where did the bowler dudes run off to? How are the McDonalds going to get home to California *now*?

To find out the answers to these and other questions, well, you'll just have to read The Genius Files #4.

ABOUT THE AUTHOR

Dan Gutman (seen here at the World of Coca-Cola) has written many books for young people, such as *Honus & Me, The Homework Machine, The Kid Who Ran For President, The Million Dollar Shot*, and the My Weird School series. If you'd like to find out about Dan or his books, visit www.dangutman.com.